Best of luck
Bob Morrissey

Humorous Beat:
Actual Funny Police Stories

by

Officer Bob Morrissey

Morrissey Publishing, Inc.
Port St. Lucie, FL 34952

Humorous Beat:
Actual Funny Police Stories

Copyright 2001 by Bob Morrissey

Published by:
Morrissey Publishing, Inc.
8286 Spicebush Terr.
Port St. Lucie, FL 34952

ISBN: 978-1-60725-883-4

Second Edition

Morrissey Publishing, Inc.
8286 Spicebush Terr.
Port St. Lucie, FL 34952

aabuckeye@comcast.net

Dedication:

To brother police officers - The brick pounders, the scout crews and detectives, who under personal peril make up the thin blue line between chaos and civilization.

Contents

Stake-Out Of The Nude Dude

Betty and Jim, a young couple, had the lights turned down watching TV when they heard the sound of bare feet slapping against the linoleum floor in the kitchen. A naked man leaped into the living room and landed in front of the television set. His back was arched, his head was pushed back, and his eyes were tightly closed. He was on his tiptoes, dancing and masturbating at the same time. He yelled, "Ya-aa-hoe" and disappeared back out of the living room as fast as he had appeared.

The young couple sat staring at each other wide-eyed. When the shock wore off Jim grabbed the phone and called the police. "Officer, you're not going to believe what I am about to tell you."

A few blocks away the nude man made his second appearance. Mabel Brown an elderly woman, was watching her TV set. She stared at him while he gyrated and put on his act. She said with a bored expression, "Honey you're not showing me much. You best go back and talk with your mama so she can make you right." Mabel, too, called the police.

The young couple's and Mabel Brown's were the first

reports to the police department. Many reports followed concerning the naked man who forced his way into homes. It discouraged the police. By the time people convinced themselves about what they had seen and called in, the nude man had made his escape. The officers searched the area but he was always gone. All they could do was write a report and forward it to the detective bureau. The detectives nicknamed the suspect the "Nude Dude." The news media picked up on the story. Every morning they'd call from as far away as New York and Los Angeles inquiring if the Nude Dude had performed the night before.

Captain John Carley, a large, tough talking man, was in charge of the investigation. Every time a report of the Nude Dude breaking into a home came into the detective bureau, he'd put a red pin in the large wall map. Many times I saw him sticking the pin into the map talking to himself. "Crazy son-of-a-bitch. I've got murders, rapists, and burglars to find and I have to waste our time on a damned nut who dances naked."

The pins soon had one section of the map almost completely red. It was time for a stake out. officers would wear civilian clothes and blend into the area where the suspect was committing most of his crimes. Stake-outs are usually boring. This one was not.

Captain Carley was standing in front of the room looking at us. "Men, I want this crazy bastard caught bad. I'm tired of him getting away with this." He pointed to the large wall map. "If you notice, there are white cards with your names on it. This is the area you will be responsible for. If we have a break-in, you will all close in on the location, keeping an eye out for this naked nut. Good hunting men."

Detective Myers muttered, "Can we call this bare hunting?"

The Captain just stared at him then said, "Skip the bull-shit, just get his naked ass behind bars."

Seeing the other detectives dressed in old clothes was different. Black sweatshirts, dark jeans, black jackets, and black hats. Even though the weather was hot we wore jackets, and gloves. We were warned that the mosquitoes in this area would attack any bare skin.

Sergeant Hurley had spread our equipment on a desk top. We strapped on revolvers, walkie-talkies, portable police radios, mace, handcuffs, flash lights, binoculars, and cans of mosquito spray. Arnold yelled out. "I feel like a pack mule."

Someone else, "I wish they'd issue knives. When we catch this slope head we could cut off his tool, then arrest him for insufficient funds." A few more wise remarks and we left for our locations in a dark unmarked car.

One by one we were dropped off in alleys that would be our section. My turn came. The car stopped, and I got out. It drove off. I stood in the middle of an alley until my eyes got accustomed to the darkness. Clouds had completely snuffed out the stars and moon. It was hot, not a breeze. I looked at a clump of bushes and weeds to my right. This would be a perfect place to conceal myself. I separated the branches and leaves, and sat down. Immediately I heard a loud buzz, then I felt like a pin cushion as my body was being bitten by insects. I swatted, scratched, and sprayed insect repellent. Nothing seemed to work. The mosquitoes must have had extensions on their stingers because they were punching through my clothes. I thought to myself, if I don't get out of here soon I'll need a blood transfusion. I made one leap and came crashing out of the bushes. I looked back and wondered to myself about this guy running around here without any clothes. I bet he looks like the map in the office with all the red pins. When we get him we'll be sure to know if he was performing around here.

Two hours passed and the only activity was the mosquitoes focusing their attack on me. I pulled a handkerchief from my pocket and wrapped it around my face and tied it in the back. Just as I settled down for a long, hot night the walkie-talkie started to crackle. In a low voice Det. Mcvay said. "Morrisey."

I pressed the button. In a whisper I answered, "Go ahead."

"I just saw a guy go into your alley. He's headed your way."

"Ok I'll watch for him and keep you advised."

I backed to a garage and waited. About five minutes later I saw a man's figure moving my way. When he got closer I saw he was staggering, and intoxicated. I pressed my back to the garage and didn't move. I hoped he would pass and not see me. As luck would have it, my dark clothes were silhouetted against the white garage. He looked my way and stood in the middle of the alley staring at me. I didn't move. He stumbled forward then gained control of himself. His eyes squinted as he looked at all the paraphernalia hanging off me and the dark handkerchief covering my face. I thought to myself, what am I going to do? How do I explain to a drunk what I'm doing?

His face was so close to mine our noses were touching. His eyes squinted and he backed away. I threw up my arms and yelled, "Boo!" At this, the man, in his clumsy retreat stumbled into the garage across the alley, and ricocheted into a group of garbage cans, sending them flying like bowling pins. He gained his bearings and disappeared into the darkness. About four houses down I saw all the lights go on after a loud bang which sounded as though he tore the door from the hinges. I wondered how he explained that to his wife.

Time passed slowly. I continued to lean against the garage. I thought to myself - I hope we get him soon, I can think of better assignments. Then I saw movement. It looked like a man crouched running into the back yard of a home. I notified the other detectives that I was going to investigate. I went to the yard stood by a tree. More movement and the figure went into some evergreens. I ran as fast as I could to the bushes. I thought I would grab him and hold him till the other officers arrived. In my dash, I tripped on a tree stump and my momentum sent me airborne. I put my hands in front of me and aimed for the moving image. Much to my surprise when I landed on the shadow, I didn't feel bare skin. I felt two armfuls of fur. From the feel of the large muscles, and the growling, I realized I was grappling with a large dog, a German Shepherd.

The only thought I had was where is the part of the body with the tail attached. I wanted to keep away from the mouth. I kept yelling, "Easy boy," while I held on to him. He in turn kept growling and snapping.

A large spotlight attached to the rear of a home went on. It lit up the yard like an arena. The dog ran in fright. I picked myself up and backed into the darkness. Det. Mcvay's voice full of laughter sounded out of the darkness. "Ride'em, cowboy."

I stood in the dark not moving. My heart slowed down. The police radio came alive. The dispatcher sent two scout crews to the home. It was just a matter of minutes when the first car pulled up. A man was standing on his front porch. "Officers, a guy was attacking a German Shepherd in my backyard."

The officers yelled. "OK, sir, we'll check it out." They came into the backyard their flashlights shining in front of them. When they got to the alley one of the detectives called to the uniformed officers. They went to the sound of the voice and in a short time returned to the lighted yard, smiling. I couldn't hear what they told the man who was waiting on his front porch but he must of been satisfied

Preface:

Police work is ongoing stress. It includes tense association with people who commit theft, murder and mayhem. It also includes the human duties of telling someone their loved ones have been maimed, killed, or arrested. Punctuating this bitterness are those precious humorous moments which make the job acceptable and keep an officer's sanity.

This book is a compilation of humorous situations which helped me cope. I believe one should judge his life on how many times he laughs. I hope my book, will make you laugh ... and help you cope..

because when they pulled away the lights went out in the back yard.

About three hours later we were picked up and brought back to the station. The other detectives were laughing. They were told about the dog. Meyers shook his head. "If you think that was bad, I was walking on my tiptoes trying not to make any noise. All at once I stepped on an alley cat that was sleeping. The only thing that moved was my bowels."

On my return to duty the second night of the stake-out I got the same assignment. This night, when I was dropped off, I thought I would be smarter. I saw a large tree with limbs extending over the alley. I climbed it and managed to get out on one of the limbs with all my dangling equipment intact. I made myself as comfortable as I could sitting on a limb. I thought this wasn't too bad. I could see the alley from both directions. The mosquitoes weren't as thick. And if that big dog returned for a rematch, no way could he get me.

Headlights from the far end of the alley pierced the darkness. A car moved slowly and the radio was playing. As it got closer I could see it was a convertible. It was hard to determine how many people were in the car since the lady was sitting so close to the driver. The car slowed and parked next to the tree directly below me. old lover boy sure had a line. The action in the front seat got hotter. I had to do something to get them out of the alley. I thought to myself, I could come off this branch and land behind the steering wheel like the Hertz advertisement, but I decided against it. I aimed my flashlight down on them and said. "Excuse me, does either of you have a light." The clothes were flying and a lot of other activity was going on in that front seat. Two screams broke the silence of the night. One from the lady and the other from the tires of the car as it sped off.

I laughed so hard I thought I'd fall off the limb. I didn't mean to scare them but I did manage to get rid of them.

Two weeks passed and we were all getting tired of the assignment. We were trying our best but the Nude Dude continued his escapades. A couple of times we were within a half block when he broke into a home. We rushed to the scene only to find that he had vanished. It was unreal.

We were so close and he always managed to get away. It was discouraging.

Captain Carley called a meeting. We just sat there while he walked back and forth in the front of the room shouting. "What the hell are we dealing with, a naked ghost? He's breaking into homes right in the middle of the stakeout. One of you guys should have seen something. Are you falling asleep out there? Were looking like a bunch of fools. Every damn newspaper in the United States is writing up this bullshit. Men, let's give this all the effort we can and find this idiot."

We went back to the stake-out. I thought I would be on this assignment till I retired. It was getting so bad I was dreaming about this naked phantom. Finally we got our break. I was sitting in the middle of the alley looking toward the end where the street-lights were on. If anyone walked into the alley he would be silhouetted. I jumped to my feet when a woman's scream pierced the silence. This was followed by a man's yell, "Ya-aa-hoe." And the sound of a door slamming.

I grabbed the walkie-talkie. "This is Morrissey. Give me back up. He just broke into a house on the even side of the ten hundred block of Euclid Street." I ran to the house where I thought the noise came from. As I opened a swinging gate to the backyard it swung right into my body. A naked man came running out. I fell backwards into the alley. I was stunned. I could see the cheeks of his ass going up and down as he was making his getaway. I jumped to my feet and gave chase. He left the alley, jumped a fence, and ran onto 1-280. Car brakes squealed as they stopped for the naked man running in front of them. I shouted into the walkie-talkie. "He just ran across 1-280 He's headed north through a field of high weeds."

I crossed the highway and walked into the neck-high weeds. I turned off the police radio and walkie-talkie. I didn't want to give my location to the Nude Dude. I didn't use my flashlight. I tried not to make noise. I walked about five feet and waited. I listened for any movement. I heard what sounded like a person exhaling hard. Slowly I made my way toward it. I raised my feet high so I would not drag weeds and make a noise. My heart jumped into my mouth

9

as my foot came down on the chest of a human body. Even though it was dark I could tell I stepped on a human. I lit my flashlight and pointed my revolver. A bearded man was looking up at me. "Hey man don't shoot. I'll give you everything I got. Just don't shoot." I turned the light to his side and there was a young girl, and another guy. They were hippies. The air reeked of marijuana smoke.

"What the hell are you people doing here?"

"Oh man, we just lay here till the sun comes up. It's a real happening when the sun comes up. That's what it's all about, man."

I could see they were stoned. "Did any of you see a naked man run through here?"

The one I stepped on replied. "Yeah man, I saw a lot of them. Every day I see about seven of them."

I shook my head and cursed under my breath. I checked on the radio to see if anyone else had seen the Nude Dude. It seemed as though he had disappeared again.

The dispatcher yelled over the radio. "We just got a call that a naked man entered a home at 707 Dearborn street."

That address was only two blocks away. I quickly ran to the house. Other detectives and uniformed crews were already there. Every light in the house was lit. A lady in a bathrobe stood in the front room with her husband who only had on a pair of undershorts. She shouted. "I thought I felt my husband's hand on me under the covers. I put my hand on the hand and I asked my husband. "When did you get a ring?" I turned on the light and this naked man was standing next to the bed doing bad things. He shouted something and ran out of the house.'

Her husband yelled. "He ought to be wet because I threw a glass of water on him."

The stake-out crew just shook their heads. I looked at them and said. "We were so close."

One of them said. "To bad one of those cars on the highway didn't smash him."

We were ready to call it a night when a car pulled up. The driver saw us in civilian clothes standing next to a marked scout car. "You guys cops? You better get over on Kelsey Street there's a woman screaming in the middle of the street with a lit railroad flare."

We rushed to Kelsey street. A red eerie glow with smoke coming from it lit up the street. A lady was holding a fusee. We yelled to her. "We're police. What's going on?"

"I bubbled his ass."

"You what?"

"I bubbled him up. A bare-ass man broke into my house. He was jumping around like a fool. I keeps this railroad flare next to my couch. I lit it up and threw some hot stuff on him. He tried to get out the window but he got stuck. I then lit up his bootee."

"Where's he at now, lady?"

"He's still stuck in the window." She pointed to the back of her home.

We ran to the rear of the home. We could hear moans

11

before we saw him. One leg was sticking out the window and the other was inside. The window was jammed down onto his shoulders. After the lady burned him with the flare she jammed a piece of wood in the sliding part of the window.

We slowly removed him. Was this was the ghost? The phantom? The guy we worked so hard to catch? The guy the news media was making into a legend? A little old lady put an end to his reign.

The Nude Dude was taken to the hospital and treated five days for intense burns. Captain Carlie put guards on him twenty-four hours a day. He was not taking any chances that the Nude Dude would escape.

Detective Mcvay and myself were assigned the follow up investigation. We went to the Record Bureau and pulled all the case reports that we thought the Nude Dude had done. There were ninety seven.

He sat in a chair in our interrogation room and stared at us when we entered. We didn't call him the Nude Dude, we used his real name. I said. "It's nice to see you in clothes, Jim." He didn't smile. I shook his hand. "You were the best we ever dealt with. I never saw a man run so fast. So many times we thought we had you. But somehow you disappeared. Jim how did you do it? Like I said, you are the best we ever dealt with."

He smiled, I felt he was going to talk. He stayed silent, then said. "I ran track in high school and made All State. But it wasn't my speed that got me away. It was my brain.

You see, I out-thought you guys."

I nodded my head. "I believe that Jim. You sure did out-smart us. Please tell us how you did it. Maybe we can help you when you go to court."

"You mean you might help me if I come clean with you?"

"I think we can. You didn't hurt anyone. You just scared hell out of them. You see all these papers? There are ninety seven reports that we think you're responsible for. I think if you tell us the truth we can clear most of these cases without you going to court for them. It all depends if you cooperate."

He thought it over for awhile. "Well, you see. I used to climb only onto flat-roofed garages. I would take off my clothes and leave them on the roof. I'd climb down and force my way into a house. When I was done I'd climb back onto the roof of the garage. I'd put my clothes back on and just lay on the roof till people started to go to work in the morning. I'd climb back down and walk home. Many a night I sat up there and laughed when you guys were running through backyards with flashlights, cussing. Not once did any of you ever look on top of a garage."

I nodded my head. "You're right, Jim, I was one of those dummies out there. Not once did we look on a garage roof."

The Dude wanted to cooperate. We handcuffed him and drove to the addresses on the reports. We asked how he entered the home, and other things he did while inside. He told us, and we checked with the report. When we were convinced he was responsible for the incident, we would clear it. Many homes he pointed out we had no reports for. We checked with the people living there and they admitted it happened but they didn't call the police. At one home he said that he didn't take off his clothes. He just went inside because he had seen a pretty lady a few days earlier go into the home. On the night he broke into this home he went into the bedroom to look at the lady. He stood next to the bed but didn't do any thing because a man was sleeping next to her. He left the house.

I went to this home and a man about twenty five years old answered. I asked him if he was aware a man had broken into his house? He had a questioning look on his face. "I'm not missing anything." I then explained to him what the Nude Dude told me. The man asked. "Was this guy wearing a construction boot with a circle on the sole of his shoe?" I went back to the car and asked the Nude Dude what the bottom of his shoe looked like? He explained there was a circle on the sole.

I again went to the home. I explained to the man, the guy who broke into his home wore the shoes he described. He grabbed his head and shouted. "Oh no, I don't believe this. I was wrong and she was right."

"What is the matter? What do you mean she was right, and you were wrong?"

"Officer, me and my wife are getting a divorce because I saw a muddy shoe print on the linoleum floor of our bedroom. This print was from a man's construction boot and in the middle of this shoe print was a circle. I don't have that kind of shoe. I accused her of being unfaithful."

I asked the man to bring his wife to the detective bureau and we would explain what the suspect told us. He said he was going to call her right away.

The Nude Dude went to court. We kept our part of the bargain. We talked to the prosecutor and the judge about how the man cooperated with us. The Nude Dude was sent to a mental hospital where he could get treatment. We all breathed a sigh of relief. Myers looked at the other guys from the stake-out crew. "Maybe if he's good the shrink will get him a free membership into a nudist colony."

BOB MORRISSEY

The Devil Got Me

A woman ran to the paddy wagon. "Help officers, there's an animal in my basement."

Officer Marty got out. "What kind of an animal? A squirrel, cat, dog.?"

"No much bigger. I heard loud noises coming from my basement. I opened the door and there was this big hairy thing with a beard down there. I didn't get a good look because I was scared. I slammed the door."

Marty looked at his partner. "What do you think Ben?"

"I think we better take a look." They walked into the home. Ben opened the door to the basement. "Damn, man, it's a big goat."

Marty looked over Ben's shoulder. "How in the hell did it get in her basement?"

"It isn't how he got in the basement. It's how in the hell are we going to get him out? Marty, do you know any thing about goats?"

"No, but I know this one's hungry. He's chewing on the steps."

Ben turned to the lady who was standing a safe distance behind them. "Mama, you got any vegetables?"

"I have a head of lettuce in the fridge." She quickly got

it. Ben threw a leaf to the goat. He caught it in his mouth and immediately swallowed it. Ben threw another leaf only this time it landed half way up the steps. The goat made one jump and had it.

Ben smiled. "He sure is hungry. Marty, hurry, go open the back doors to the wagon."

Ben held the head of lettuce in front of him waving it back an forth so the goat could see it. Doing this, he backed out of the house and the goat followed. When he got to the wagon he threw the lettuce inside. The goat jumped in and Ben slammed the doors.

The lady thanked them and they drove off. Ben took the mike from the cradle. "Dispatcher, this is Unit Ten. We got a goat in the back of our wagon and we're on the way to the animal shelter."

"This is the dispatcher. You got what in the back of your wagon?"

"We got a goat and were taking it to the animal shelter."

"This is the dispatcher. Disregard that goat. We got a priority emergency call. Go to First, and Main St. Cover an ambulance call at the church. The preacher is unconscious and has to be taken to the hospital immediately."

"Dispatcher this is Unit Ten. Did you copy? We have a goat in the back of our wagon. What are we going to do with the thing?"

"Unit Ten get the goat out of your wagon and come back for it later. Take the ambulance call. Get the man to the hospital."

Marty pulled over to the curb. "What are we going to do Ben?"

"We do what the man said. Get the damn goat out of the wagon and take the ambulance run."

They opened the back doors. The goat stared at them. Ben shook his head. "This is going to be fun. Marty you grab one horn and I'll grab the other one and we'll pull it out." They grabbed his horns and the goat quickly lowered his head and spread its front legs. The officers couldn't budge him.

Marty cussed under his breath. "Come on you nanny-goat bastard. I'll bring you a whole head of lettuce when we come back if you cooperate." No matter how hard they tried the goat would not move.

The radio came alive again. "Unit Ten this is the dispatcher how close are you to the church? Step it up. The man needs help."

Hearing this, Ben slammed the back doors. "Screw the dispatcher and this fur faced goat. Let's get going we'll make the ambulance run with the damn thing."

Ben jumped from the paddy wagon and shouted. "Marty, get the stretcher. I'll go inside the church and see what's going on."

Marty crawled over the goat and got the stretcher. He ran down the aisle of the church and laid the stretcher next to where Ben was kneeling by a man dressed in a black robe. Ben looked up at Marty. "He's unconscious but he's

19

breathing. Let's get him to the hospital." They lifted him on to the stretcher and were carrying him from the church when one of the ladies ran up and put a straw hat on his chest.

"This is the reverend's. He don't go nowhere without it."

The stretcher with the preacher was placed on the floor of the Paddy Wagon. Ben got in the back with the preacher. Marty drove. The goat stared at the preacher's hat. His mouth clamped down on it. Ben tried to get it away but the goat devoured it. Ben shook his head and shouted. "Ain't this a bitch. I don't believe this is happening."

Ben's loud yell must have caused the preacher to regain conscious. His eyes blinked a few times then came wide open. The goat's face with it's long beard was just inches away from his.

The preacher screamed."Oh lordie. It's the devil! I'm sorry I should of never messed with Mrs. Brown, Ruby, Martha or all those other women from the congregation. Oh I didn't mean it. Don't let this devil carry me to Hell."

Marty slid the window open. "Ben, what's going on back there?"

"The preacher thinks he died and believes the devil's got him. He's making his confession."

The Last Fling

A rookie policeman learns many things that aren't in the manual; and most of them come from your first veteran partners.

My first partner was Dick Marko, and he had my full attention. At first I respected him because he was an ex-marine who'd seen combat in Korea, and I had to respect that. Soon I looked up to him for his approach to police work even more.I was young and eager, and thought a policeman's job was to enforce the law and make arrests, but under his tutelage I quickly learned there was a better side to it. He was relaxed and slow to anger. He was strangely sensitive to the inhabitants of our beat, which included Toledo's notorious Summit-Cherry Streets corner. He kept the peace in a most peaceful manner, and everybody liked him. He even made his arrests as peaceable as possible.What I remember most was not an arrest. It was the time we picked up an old gent, a walkaway from one of the nursing homes. They'd told us to be on the lookout for him at roll call. It was one of a long list of things they read off.

We checked out our scout car and were crossing

Cherry Street when Dick elbowed me and said. "Over there." There ahead of us was an old man in a worn-out robe and old bedroom slippers. It undoubtedly was the walkaway. He spotted us over his shoulder and took off running. His bathrobe flew open and he lost a slipper, but he kept going.

I pulled up next to him. Dick rolled down the window, and shouted, "Hey, pop. Do you know where Summit Street is?"

Skip the bull," the guy shouted back. "I know what you guys are up to." He kept on running.

Dick told me to pull up a little ahead of him. The guy turned around and went the other way. We got out of the car and jogged after him. He stopped, and turned on us with clenched fists.

"If you want your butts kicked, keep messing with me," he challenged.

Dick gave him a big friendly smile. "Hold it. We don't want to fight with you. We just want to help you."

The old gent's eyes flashed. "Help me, my ass. You just want to take me back to the damn nursing home. I'm not going, so just shove off. I'm 90 years old. I did a hitch in the Marines, and then I was a sailor for the rest of my life. I'm not meant for that place. I've been there for five years, and the only excitement I ever get is watching the spit run down some guy's chin. Hell, I haven't even had a drink since I went in there.

Dick drew up almost to attention, looked right at the

old gent, and asked earnestly, "Would you lie to a fellow marine?"

"Hell, no. I wouldn't lie to a fellow marine. I'd die for a fellow marine," he replied.

"Well, pop, I was in the marines, and I feel the same way you do. I'll make a deal. If you don't fight us we'll take you to a place that is full of life and we'll get you some drinks."

The old man hesitated, "This ain't no trick?"

"It's no trick," Dick assured him as he opened the rear door of the scout car. You could see the doubt in the old fellow's face, but he got in.

I got behind the wheel and looked to Dick for directions.

"Summit and Cherry," he said. "Highway Bar."

Then Dick turned to the back seat and said. "Now I trust you, pop, and I think you trust me. We are going to drop you off at the Highway Bar. You stay there, and we'll be back at 10 o'clock to pick you up. You don't leave the bar. Is that a deal?"

"It's a deal," the old man said. Dick reached back and the two shook hands. I was pretty nervous about this. "Should I tell the dispatcher?" I asked, reaching for the radio. "Won't we be out of service?"

"Just drive, Bob." he replied. Then he turned to the guy. "This will be our little secret, right, pop?"

You could hear the smile in the guy's voice. "Whatever you guys say. It's too late in the game for me."

23

I pulled up at the bar, and Dick helped the man out of the car. The old fellow shuffled up to the window, and cupped his eyes so he could see inside. "This is my kind of place," he said approvingly.

Dick reached into his wallet, pulled out a $5 bill, folded it up and slipped it in a pajama pocket. He motioned to me, and I did the same thing. Hey, I was the rookie, he was the teacher.

As we opened the door, music and odors wafted out at us. The old guy was glowing.

The man who ran the place, Sandy something, came over to find out what two cops and an old guy in pajamas and robe wanted. Dick knew him, of course. He knew everybody in the neighborhood, it seemed.

I didn't want to stray too far from our radio, but I saw this Sandy guy take the old fellow by the arm and lead him into the place. "He'll be fine." Dick assured me when he returned to the car. "Let's get out of here."

I didn't feel too good about this, and kept thinking that we ought to pick the guy up again and take him back to the home where he belonged. "The place is full of prostitutes and other undesirables, and once he pulls those two fives out of his pocket he's dead," I argued.

"Don't worry," he argued back. "This is his homecoming. They're his kind of people. He'll take care of himself."

He'd been in there maybe four hours, closer to five and I was counting the minutes. At last Dick told me to head for the Highway Bar again. "Go in and get him," he said, smiling.

I opened the door. The room was nothing but action, loud music, talking, laughing, and smoke. You could hardly breathe with all that smoke, let alone see. Finally, I picked him out. It took a little while. He was surrounded by women -- women of the night, but women. His bathrobe and top of his pajamas were draped over a nearby chair. At first I was going to grab him and hurry him out of there, but he was having the time of his life bragging about his tattoos.

"This one," he said, touching his shoulder gently, "I got in Hong Kong. I found this pretty women and we had a night. When I woke up I had this beautiful tattoo. Every time I get lonely I rub it and think of that pretty lady and that great night."

The girls were all over him, laughing at everything he said and seeing that he wanted for nothing in the line of cigarettes, smokes or drinks. Then I noticed Dick standing behind me. He listened for a while and then reached over and tapped the old gent.

"Marine, it's time for taps," he said.

The old guy stopped his story telling, slowly rose from the chair, brought himself to attention, and replied in a low voice. "Yes, sir." Slowly he picked up his pajama top, and then his bathrobe. Everything in the room stopped --- the noise, the laughter, even the music.

The women began helping him dress. One turned on us. "Let him stay here," she said. "We can take good care of him, better than where you're taking him."

The idea seemed to appeal to the old man. He looked at Dick for some kind of approval, but Dick shook his head negatively. I could swear, though, that tears were welling up in Dick's eyes. "Come on, pop," he said gently. "You promised no fighting."

"It would take more cops than you've got here," the guy said, and then turned to the women. "I gave my word as a Marine. You are beautiful ladies, but I have to go with my friends." He shuffled toward the door.

We had some Kleenex in the car. Dick offered him a sheet. "You've got some lipstick on your neck," he explained.

The old guy shoved Dick's hand away. "I'll keep it there," he said, smiling. "Wait till the old broads at the nursing home see it. I'll never wash it off."

"Let's go home," Dick said. I headed for the nursing home.

We drove in silence for awhile, and then the old guy pulled our two five-dollar bills from his pajama pocket and offered them to Dick. "They wouldn't let me spend anything," he said.

"Keep it," Dick replied.

"What the hell am I going to do with it in the home?" He growled. "Buy yourself a few drinks. Have some on the old man you made very happy."

Dick took the money. "The drinks will be on you pop" he agreed. They shook hands.

When we pulled up to the nursing home door there was a nurse or aid or something waiting for him. "Mr. Wilcox," she said. "We're glad to see you. You had us worried."

She reached in to help the guy out of the car. He put his arms around her neck. "Hello, baby," he laughed.

She wrestled free. "He smells like a brewery," she cried glaring at us.

Dick shrugged his shoulders. "We picked him up on Skid Row."

I don't know if the guy was kidding or whether he actually passed out, but we had to help her get him to his bed, unconscious or not, I swear he was grinning.

The woman thanked us for the help. "I'm sorry, officers, that he caused you a problem."

"He was no problem," Dick assured her.

Then we drove away, and I had a brand new idea of what police work can be.

BOB MORRISSEY

JOHN'EN

The Officers are called to attention. Sgt. Lewis, standing in front of the men, begins Roll Call. He shouts out a name and an officer responds, "Here, Sir." He puts down the roster board and is about to read the daily scoop when the door opens and Captain Grady walks in.

"Hold it Sergeant!"

Someone in ranks mumbles, "Oh shit, he's looking for a John."

Captain Grady is the head of the Vice Squad. He's a powerfully - built man and a tough cop. He's from the old school. He knows every four-letter word ever uttered. He will never forget them because he uses them every day.

We all know what he wants. A new face. A uniform officer to put on civilian clothes and work under cover. Better known as John'en.

The Captain slowly makes his way through the formation. When he spots a new uniform he stops and stares. He knows a new uniform usually means a rookie; thus, a new face. The officers give a sigh of relief after he gives them the once over and moves on.

I sense him coming closer to me. Seeing my new

uniform, he stops. He squints his eyes as he looks at me. He sticks his finger into my chest. "You'll do, get some civies on!"

I make a face - "Why me?"

"Because I'm looking for someone with a ugly baby face who those bastards on the street would never guess we would hire for a policeman." Everyone laughs. The Captain hits me on the shoulder. "Get with it kid."

I change clothes and hesitantly walk into the Vice Squad office. A couple of veteran detectives saw me and laughed. One of them said, "Fresh Meat."

Captain Grady points to a desk, "Sit your ass down." I do. He hovers over me and shouts. "What you got against working plain clothes, This is where you learn. Don't you want to be taught?"

I look up at him and stare straight into his eyes. "The last time I got one of your lessons, I learned how to get a beer bottle broken over my head, get kicked in the privates, and how many shots I had to take when I got bitten by that two-hundred-and-fifty pound whore whose teeth almost broke my arm. I worried for two weeks thinking I could've caught rabies, or hoof-and-mouth disease."

He laughs. "Tonight it will be different. There won't be any rough stuff. The last time we were dealing with a smart street walker. Who would have ever thought she would take you into one apartment building then walk out the back door into a alley. Then go into another building. We were out front waiting for you."

"Yeah, you were out front of the wrong building. I was in a room with the big whore, her pimp, and another guy. I didn't have a gun because you guys said she would feel for the gun and would know I was a cop. Luck'ly I faked them out. They thought I had a gun when I pulled my badge and arrested that big woman. She fought me like a wild elephant. I'm wearing my gun tonight - no matter what."

"Now listen to me kid." All I want you to do is go into the Cherry Street Restaurant at three o'clock when the bars close and buy a coffee. You know where the Cherry Street Restaurant is?"

"Yes, I know where the Cherry Street Restaurant is. It's one of those dirty joints on skid row. You know, Captain, if you want that place shut down, all you have to do is give the Health Department a call."

"No, we're going to take it down. They're serving whiskey without a license. Here's how it works. You go in and sit at the counter. Coffee is only forty-five cents. If you want a shot of whiskey in your coffee you put two dollars down. The owner will take the two dollars and get you a coffee with whiskey in it. Now, you got how it works?"

"Yes, I get the coffee with the whiskey in it, then I show my badge and arrest him. I got one question Captain. What happens when the fireworks start?"

"What you mean the, fireworks?"

"You know that's a tough joint. When I pull my badge all hell is going to break out. It'll be three in the morning and everyone in the place will be drunk out of his mind."

31

"I told you. We'll be watching every move you make. As soon as you pull the badge. We'll rush in. There will be no problem."

I reluctantly get into the Captain's unmarked car, a dark-green Ford. We didn't talk till he parked in a dark spot in an alley, facing Cherry Street. The rain had stopped and car lights were reflecting off the wet pavement on Cherry Street. Captain Grady was giving me last minute instructions. I listened to him but my attention was interrupted when I heard the loud noise of a door banging open. Two drunks staggered into the alley from the side door of a cheap bar. One, a tall woman, and the other a short man. They were laughing and talking loud. The woman leaned up against the building and the guy was standing in front of her. We could see everything they were doing since they were silhouetted against the lights on Cherry Street. They talked for a brief time, and the man took out his wallet and gave her some money. She partly disrobed, and so did he.

I looked over at the Captain. "Hey, do you see what they're doing?"

"Hell, yes, I see what they're doing. She's turning a Five Dollar Trick. He won't get his money's worth because she's too tall and he's too short. Someone's gotta put him up to it. Never mind that bullshit, We want to bust that restaurant."

I didn't say anymore because he really didn't give a damn. I kept watching them. The short guy would go forward bump into the big woman lose his balance and stagger backwards and both of them would cuss. This went on for awhile. The guy got discouraged and he pointed to the ground. I heard her shout, "Hell no, it's wet." The short guy was now looking for a dry spot. All at once he pointed to our car.

They were now headed our way. Captain Grady saw them coming. He said in a low voice, "Scoot down, don't let them see us."

I eased down, but I could see them in front of the car putting their hands on the hood. The guy said, "It's dry this is perfect." They both crawled onto the hood.

The car was now rocking. I whispered to the Captain. "I don't believe what is going on out there."

"Just stay down and be quiet. I'm going to give them a couple of minutes. I'll take care of this."

"Hey Captain, I've got a question."

"What the hell do you want now?"

"What would happen if the Deputy Chief drove by and saw this?"

"The hell with the Deputy Chief. just be quiet. I'm going to give this guy his money's worth."

I just sat there. I felt he's the Captain let him run the show. They never taught us what to do about a situation like this in the academy.

I saw the Captain's hand slowly going for the toggle switch that activates the siren. A loud shrill wail from under the hood blasted. The participants became airborne. The man's legs were running while he was still in the air.

He hit the ground and immediately tried to get as much distance as he could from our car. His pants were wrapped around his knees. He fell and crawled as fast as he could.

The big woman rolled her hands into fists. "You perverted sons of bitches get out of that car and I'll mop this alley up with you."

The Captain stuck his head out the window. "What you all excited about, Small Change. Looks like business is good tonight."

"Oh, It's you Captain Grady? How have you been. I was just having a little fun."

"Well, Small Change, you better get out of here. This is no place for a nice lady like you to be."

"OK, Captain, thanks for the advice. Anything you say."

Hot Pursuit

Both officers were exhausted from the many calls they had answered on their tour. It was time to get off and go home. Their hats were pushed to the back of their heads, neckties pulled down, and the top button on their shirts opened. The driver, Doug, looked over to his partner. "Bill this midnight shift is a killer. I can't wait to get this car back to the station and turn it over to the day shift."

Bill's eyes flickered open and he mumbled. "Un hun." The driver kept talking and every once in awhile his partner automatically bobbed his head forward, blinked his eyes and said "Yeah, yeah."

The one-way conversation continued until the tranquillity was broken by squealing tires, and blaring car horns. Doug looked in the rearview mirror and shouted, "Bill, wake up, We got a crazy coming up behind us weaving in and out of traffic, forcing people off the road."

Bill straightened up. His eyes caught the blur, of a car passing them on the right side. He jumped to the middle of the seat as it narrowly missed the scout car. He shouted. "Get that son of a bitch, he's going to kill somebody."

Doug activated the over head red lights, and siren and pushed the gas pedal to the floor. The acceleration forced the officers back into their seats. Bill grabbed the mike from the cradle. "Dispatcher this is unit # Ten. Were in a high speed pursuit with a 1987 Blue Olds Ohio license 2A-(Able) 349 headed south on 1-280 at Manhattan Blvd. Speed in excess of Ninety Miles Per Hour."

The dispatcher acknowledged. "Ok Unit Ten, we copy. Keep us informed of your location. All units in the area assist unit Ten."

Doug concentrated on the speeding car. He maneuvered in and out of the traffic staying right on its tail. Bill had one hand on the dash board for support and the other was squeezing the mike. He started to inform the dispatcher of their new location when the speeding car crossed two traffic lanes and struck a culvert. A cloud of dust and dirt exploded from under the speeding car. It was out of control and went airborne.

The driver fought the steering wheel trying to gain control. The car came down with the wheels locked to the right. It nose dived, and the rear-end sprang up, flipped twice and landed on its roof. Sparks flew as it slid and spun from one side of the highway to the other. The car slammed into a utility pole and sheared it. The airborne pole narrowly missed the pursuit car. Wires, spitting sparks, bounced off its hood.

The speeding car flipped on its side and continued sliding with smoke and sparks erupting where metal met pavement. It came to an abrupt stop when it slammed into the metal and concrete supports of the overpass.

Both officers jumped from their car and were met by a cloud of dust, steam and smoke. They waved their hands in front of their faces to clear the air. Small pieces of broken glass sparkled on the street. When the officers ran over it, it made a crackling grinding sound. Reaching the wrecked car, which was lying on its side, they started to climb up on it to get the driver.

A man's head slowly came out of a broken window. Both officers shouted. "Are you hurt?"

He slowly shook his head, and with one eye open, slurred. "Naaaaa."

Doug shouted, "Are you drunk?"

The man's neck stiffened, his eyes came wide open and his head nodded up and down. He blurted out in a slurred voice. "Hell, yes, I'm drunk. What do you think I am, a stunt driver?"

BOB MORRISSEY

Midnight Salesman

Two men hunched over a bar making small talk, laughing and wiping the moisture from their beer glasses, suddenly became serious.

"You know what busts my backside, Jim? That siding salesman who calls every night about dinner time or in the middle of a football game. I'll bet he's called a dozen times in the last month. I don't want to buy siding. I can't get rid of him, but he keeps right on talking."

"Yea, Carl, he's a pain-in-the-butt alright, but Eddy's wife is worse. I been boiling all day about her. I wanted to talk to Eddy yesterday. His wife answered the phone. "Who are you? What do you want with Eddie;" he mocked.

"That set me off, so I answered, Good God, woman are you a warden? Do I need to pass a test to reach Eddie? I only wanted to talk with him, not get him pregnant. She went into a rage and called me names I've never even heard of. What a witch! If you want an education you aught'ta call Eddy sometime."

Rubbing his chin, Carl stood up. "Yea, I just might do that. Let's get 'em-----the both of 'em. Tonight." As he fished in his pocket for change, he said, "Hand me that phone book on the end of the bar."

"Now, what was the name of that siding company? Oh yea! "Beauregard Siding." There can't be too many Beauregard families here. Yep! John Beauregard," and he wrote the number on a napkin. He looked up Eddy's number and also wrote it on the napkin. Then went to the payphone and deposited money.

"You ain't going to call at two in the morning are you?"

"Can you think of a better time?"

The phone box digested two coins, and with the phone to his ear he dialed the number.

Jim shook his head in disbelief.

"Man that woman is going to come unglued."

Carl looked at Jim and placed his finger up to his lips motioning for quiet. He then winked indicating that she answered. Jim edged his head next to Carl's to hear the conversation.

"Hun! Hello. HELLO." It was a woman's voice.

After a moment, Carl replied, "Ma'am I'm your friendly siding salesman and I'm running a sale on aluminum siding this month, I'm calling to see if you want to take advantage of this cash saving?"

"YOU'RE WHAT? DO YOU KNOW WHAT TIME IT IS?"

"Yes Ma'am I realize it's two-fifteen in the morning, but I work nights. I can contact more people at home in the early hours of the morning. I want you also to know Ma'am that we will put your siding on at two, or three in the morning if you take advantage of this cash saving deal."

"LISTEN YOU IDIOT, IF I HAD YOU BY YOUR DAMN THROAT YOU WOULDN'T BE CALLING ANY MORE PEOPLE AT THIS HOUR OF THE MORNING."

"But you don't understand ma'am. I like the midnight shift. After a while, you get used to it."

"NOW YOU LISTEN YOU BASTARD, AFTER I CALL THE BETTER BUSINESS BUREAU YOU WON'T BE WORKING THE MIDNIGHT SHIFT ANY-MORE."

"But listen lady you don't understand. I got to make a living like everyone else."

"IF YOU EVER CALL THIS HOUSE AGAIN, YOU IGNORANT, STUPID JERK, I'LL SEARCH YOU OUT AND BREAK YOUR DAMN NECK."

"Look ma'am, I won't be calling you anymore, but the first thing this morning at about eight thirty I'll be over with my samples and I'm sure that after you see my product, and the price you'll be glad I contacted you."

"YOU BETTER NOT COME ON MY PORCH OR THEY'LL BE CARRYING YOU OFF FEET FIRST, BUSTER." With a sharp click, the other end of the phone went dead.

Jim looked at Carl. "See what did I tell you? Did you hear that language? Ain't she a beaut?"

Carl shook his head and smiled. "Man, that woman is

tough. She's really burning. No wonder old Eddie asks how high, when she says jump."

Then Carl dialed his second number.

"Wha-what is happening? What do you want?"

"Mr. John Bureauregard of Bureauregard Siding?"

"Yes."

"Mr. Beauregard, I just got orders to ship out in the morning. You've called me many times. I need to sell my house and I believe that with aluminum siding it will sell better. I must leave now, but will you meet my wife at eight-thirty in the morning and show her your samples? If the price is right we'll pay cash for the job."

The man on the other end automatically started his sales pitch, but Carl interrupted him. "Listen Sir, if you will tell my wife the details, I'm sure she will understand and will listen. The address is twelve ten Baker Street. But you gotta be here by eight-thirty, because my wife is leaving at nine. Can you make it?"

"Oh yes, I'll come out there myself."

"That's great, we'll pay cash if the deal is right." Carl hung up the phone and smiled.

At eight-forty-five in the morning, the police radio came alive. "Unit 12! Step it up. We have a demented woman in a bath robe. She's swinging a broom and chasing a man down the twelve hundred block of Baker Street."

"Unit 12, OK, were on the way."

No one paid much attention to the two men laughing in the car across the street from twelve ten Baker Street.

Heart Attack

Roy and I were partners for ten years, three in the uniform section and seven in the detective bureau. Not only was he my partner he was a good friend. I was a little younger, and smaller then Roy. We got into some bad scrapes but somehow managed to escape injury. Yet to this day I still wonder how we made it. Many times we were outnumbered but fought our way out. I must confess Roy did most of the fighting. He was about six two, and two hundred and thirty pounds. Before coming on the police force he was a professional boxer. He fought some of the best fighters. His career stopped one night when he hit his opponent so hard he knocked him out, but Roy broke every bone in his hand.

Roy became a police officer, but he continued being active in sports. He was one of the top professional bowlers in the state. Every morning after work he bowled at least ten games. He was tough but he never bullied anyone. He would take a lot but when someone backed him into a corner and tried to get physical Roy would make short work of the guy.

He was the perfect partner except he had one flaw. He was too good looking. Everything in a skirt chased him. It wasn't a long chase. Roy saw to that. He was divorced six times and was in the process of another one.

On many occasions we were investigating crimes in the seedy part of town. Ladies of the night would see Roy and say, "Whew, eeee, baby, you can arrest me any time." Roy used this to our advantage. He would take them to the side and give them that sweet talk he was so good at. It was just a short time and she was telling him everything he wanted to know. We made a lot of important arrests due to Roy's talent. One night about three in the morning, we had completed an investigation when I heard a grunting noise from the passenger seat where Roy was sitting. I saw him bent over hugging his chest. His face showed pain. I shouted, "What's the matter Roy?"

"Bob, I think I'm having a heart attack."

We're close to Creekside Hospital. Hold on, I'll be there in a couple of minutes."

"No Bob, not Creekside."

"Why? It's right around the corner. It's a good hospital.

"No Bob, I messed over a few of them nurses there. Sure as hell if they get the chance they'll pull the plug."

I laughed. "OK Roy we'll go to St. Andrews. It's farther but if it makes you feel better that's where we'll go."

"Thanks Bob, that's where I want to go. You do me an important favor?"

"Sure Roy, just name it."

"Bob, if I pass out will you get me a good doctor? This is serious and I want the best. A lot of these guys don't know what the hell they're doing. I don't want one of those dummies working on me."

"Don't worry Roy, I'll be with you all the time. I'll see to it that you get the best." I parked the car under the awning to the emergency room. I looked over at him. "Roy, I'll be right back with the orderlies and a stretcher."

"No Bob, I want to walk in."

The nurse in the emergency room saw us come through the door. She looked at Roy bent over holding his chest and the painful expression on his face. She quickly ran to us and grabbed his arm and directed us to a guerney. Roy crawled up on it and leaned back. He stared at me with a serious look like I never saw before. "Remember what you promised me Bob."

"I remember. Now lay back and take it easy."

I heard footsteps coming our way. I looked down the hall and saw this man dressed in a white gown that hung below his waist. His pants were baggy knickers and he wore sandals. A turban was wrapped around his head. He had a long beard, and a stethoscope wrapped around his neck. He stopped in front of me. Roy looked at him and I heard him say. "Aw man, shit."

The doctor pointed at Roy and said to me in broken English. "What a matter him?"

I pointed at Roy. "Ask him, he's the guy who needs

45

help."

I could tell he didn't understand a word I said. He got a mean look on his face and shouted. "What a matter him?"

I got mad at his tone. I looked him straight in the eyes and shouted. "He wants to get circumcised."

Roy's eyes came wide open. "Oh man don't jive this silly son of bitch. I'm going to die for sure."

The doctor was shouting. "I no circumcise, three o'clock morning. Emergency, emergency only. He was shaking his head so hard the turban almost flew off. He grabbed Roy's jacket and started to pull him off the guerney. Roy's coat came open exposing his shoulder holster and revolver. The doctor immediately let go and a frighten look came over his face. Roy pointed at him.

"You better understand this. Heart attack, heart attack." He then pointed at his chest and back at the doctor. "Now get to work."

Roy was admitted to the hospital for three days. He never lost consciousness. He took care of the doctor problem himself. The examinations proved he pulled a muscle in his chest. It probably was caused by bowling too many games.

When Roy returned to work he walked into the squad room. All eight detectives had towels wrapped around their heads. In unison they all shouted. "What a matter you."

I can't tell you what Roy said.

Is That All You Remember?

The big game was finally going to be played South High against Westwood. Both teams were undefeated. The newspapers were giving this game a lot of coverage. South High School had a good quarterback who could really throw the ball. On the other end of the passes was Jack Murphy. Murphy was known to catch anything that was near him. As a junior he made both the All City Team and the All State team. He set all kinds of school records in football. He was having a great senior year and colleges were already offering him scholarships.

Westwood had a bigger stronger team than South. If they could stop Murphy from catching passes, Westwood could win the game. Their game plan was to rough up Jack Murphy every time he went out for a pass. Murphy felt this would be Westwood's strategy because other teams did the same thing. He didn't let this bother him. When the game started they tried to strong arm him. He was catching the ball with one hand and three defenders hanging on him. They couldn't stop him.

Murphy was playing a great game, but the score was

still 0 to 0. It was now the fourth quarter and time was quickly running off the clock. South High quarterback threw the ball to Murphy three times right across the middle. Murphy caught all three. In the huddle the quarter back looked at Murphy. "Murph you ran the same pattern for the last three plays. Their defensive half back is coming up quick on you. He probably thinks we're going to run the same pattern. This time go across the middle. I'll fake like I'm going to throw the ball to you. Put your hands up as if you're going to catch it. Then stop and run into the end zone and turn around. I'll throw the pass to you, and we'll score." Murphy as usual didn't say anything. He just nodded that he understood.

The play worked perfectly. Murphy ran across the middle. The quarterback pumped the ball as if he was going to throw it. Murphy raised his arms as though he was going to catch a pass. Westwood's defensive halfback thought that the quarterback threw the ball. He rushed to block it. Murphy stopped but the defensive halfback couldn't. Murphy was now alone. He ran into the end zone and turned around. The ball came at him with a tight spiral. The stadium became silent. All eyes were on the lone player in the end zone. Jack Murphy guided the ball between his arms. When it hit his chest he grasped it. The ball bounced off his chest and dribbled to his knee and onto the ground. The South High fans groaned. Cheers erupted from the Westwood stands.

Jack Murphy put his hands on his hips. His eyes

watered. He stared at the ball lying on the ground and thought. How could it have gotten away. I was standing there all alone and I dropped it. He slowly went back to the huddle. No one said anything. Everyone knew that Jack was a great player and this type of thing happens to the best. The game ended in a tie. Jack Murphy went on to be a star in college.

Fifty years later, on Mother's day Jack Murphy was in the Blooming Flower Shop buying flowers for his mother. He felt a tap on his shoulder. He turned around and faced a man. "You remember me, Jack?"

"Sure Ben, you were one of the best guards I ever played with. Man, it's been fifty years since South High."

"It sure has. Hey Murph, remember that pass you dropped in the Westwood game when you were standing all by yourself in the end zone?"

"Ben, you son of a bitch," Murphy shouted. "Is that all you remember about me? That stinking dropped pass?" Jack Murphy punched him right on the chin sending him reeling into a rose display.

"The police car radio crackled. "Units # 4 and 5. Go to the Blooming Flower Shop at 1210 Suder. Two elderly men fist fighting causing a lot of damage in the store." Unit #4 was the first to arrive at the flower shop. They could hear cussing and glass being broken. They rushed inside. Two gray haired men were wrestling, and punching one another. The officers quickly separated them. They shook their heads when they saw how old these men were. The officers had to hold them apart. They knew from the anger on these men's faces they were not done fighting. one of the officers yelled. "What are you two fighting about? There's no need for this."

Jack Murphy shouted. "I'll tell you what we're fighting about. Over fifty years ago we played football together. He saw me catch hundreds of passes. I played my heart out in those football games. I never quit I tried my best to make my team a winner. I made All State, and All City. I went on to college and played great ball. So what does this guy remember? The one stinking pass I dropped. Officers I have been living with this for all those years. Every time I see someone who went to school with me, they always say. 'Hey Jack remember that pass you dropped in the Westwood game.' These clowns will not let me forget. Tell me, officer, why can't someone come up to me and say something good I did? Oh hell, just arrest me I punched him first."

Ben put out his hand. "Jack you're not the one who started this fight. I should of known better. It just slipped out. I don't know why. I didn't think. You deserved to punch me. I know what you've been living with." The men shook hands, smiled and rubbed their chins .and congratulated each other on how they still could go.

Seeing this, the officers knew the fight was over.

The officers pointed to all the smashed flowers, and glass on the floor. Jack, and Ben took their wallets out and went to the owner who was standing behind the cash register.

As the officers walked back to their car, one said to the other, "I bet that's the most flowers this shop has ever sold."

BOB MORRISSEY

Nickel Burn

Lieutenant Fisher, a twenty-year veteran, was the
assignment officer. He was going over the police reports
from the last twenty four hours. He'd stare at a report then
pitch it into a pigeon hole with a detective's name on it.
He'd been doing this for so long he didn't have to look at
the name on the box. He stopped abruptly and slowly shook
his head when he saw the title on the report he was holding
in his hand. It read, "Injured man deep penetrating burn."
This report was almost the same M.O. as seven others he
had read in the past two weeks. The burn was the size of a
nickel and went deep into the body. In all cases the burn
was on the mens' buttocks. Nowhere did it mentioned the
men's clothes were burned. They had to have had their
pants off when they were injured. These burns must have
been serious since the injured men went to the hospital to
be treated. Not one of the victims explained how they
received these burns. They all stated it was an accident and
did not wish an investigation.

Lt. Fisher went to the record bureau and pulled the
other reports concerning injured men with nickel-size
burns. The only reason reports were filed was because the
hospital reports these incidents to the police. It's a law that

when-a person comes in for treatment and there are suspicious circumstances, the hospital must contact the police.

Lieutenant Fisher looked up the records of the victims. The only thing similar was they were all married men and were between twenty-five and thirty years old. The incidents all happened during the night hours. The more he read, the stranger it got. Even though the reports stated that no investigation was needed, he took copies of them which now numbered ten.

When he got back to the detective bureau he walked to my desk. He laid the reports down. I stared at them and looked up at him. "Hey, Lieutenant, give me a break, I'm working on twenty-four cases already."

"I'm not assigning you these reports. I only want you to look them over. They got me baffled and I don't know what is going on. Read them and tell me what you think. I'll be back in a half hour."

I read the reports and I too thought it was strange. Everyone burned on the buttocks. Not one mentioned how it happened. I couldn't imagine anyone doing this to himself. My curiosity was running rampant. Lt. Fisher came back. "Well, what do you make of it?"

"Boy, I don't know. Maybe it's some type of cult and the scar is a way to recognize the members. Man, that must have been painful to get a deep burn like that."

In the following weeks more reports were filed. Lt. Fisher would always give me a chance to read them. I, along with the other Homicide Detectives got caught up in these strange incidents. Everybody in the squad pitched in five dollars toward a pot. Whoever solved these cases would be given the money.

I was fortunate to win the pot two weeks later. The mystery was solved at three o'clock in the morning on the seedy side of town. A uniform crew was driving slowly in a rundown business district. They had the car head lights out and were playing the spotlight on store windows looking for break-ins. The car came to an abrupt halt when the silence was pierced by a shrill scream. The officer with the spotlight aimed it in the direction of the noise. A naked man came jumping and dancing out of a dark alley holding his buttocks. The officers ran to him and tried to calm him down. He kept shouting. "The bitch got me." An ambulance was called and he was transported to Lawnview Hospital.

At the other end of the alley a woman, beaten and badly bruised, crawled out and dropped on the side walk. A motorist saw her and called the police. She was taken to St. Marks Hospital.

The dispatcher sent me to the hospital where the woman had been taken. I walked into the emergency room and the nurse pointed to one of the treatment stalls. I pulled the curtain back and went in. Right away I recognized her.

It was Crazy Annie, a prostitute. She was a friendly girl always joking and smiling. I always liked her, regardless of what she was. No matter how rough she had it, she never let it get her down. Her eyes were almost swollen shut. Her lips were lacerated and blood seeping out. The rest of her body was bruised. I had to laugh when I read the tattoo which was below her belly button. "Pay Before Entering."

"What happened Annie? Who did this to you?"

She moaned a little and smiled. "Forget it Detective. It goes with the job." I don't want to prosecute even if you catch him."

"Listen Annie you don't have to prosecute. Give me his name. No one has the right to do this to you. Just let me talk with him."

She didn't answer and just looked at me with a grin. A nurse came into the room. "Detective, you're wanted on the phone."

I answered, and it was a uniform officer at Lawnview Hospital. "Detective, were taking a report of a man with a bad burn on his buttocks and I think this case is related to yours. The burned guy says he picked up a prostitute and parked in an alley. When they got going he didn't know she pressed in the cigarette lighter in the dash board and when it was red hot she rammed it into the cheek of his ass. He said it hurt so bad he lost it and beat her."

I looked down at Annie. "Tell me why you burned that guy with that lighter? I've got his side of the story now I want yours. Tell me Annie!"

She hesitated and slowly shook her head. "Well, I saw this western. The cowboys were branding cattle. It gave me a good idea. I thought if I branded my customers and they showed me the brand the next time we do business I would give them a break on the price. This guy tonight didn't like getting branded and he worked me over."

This investigation didn't go to court since neither party would prosecute. When I collected the pot money, Lt. Fisher shook his head and laughed. "Those guys are going to be lucky if all they got from crazy Annie was a brand."

BOB MORRISSEY

A Cover UP

Jerry Rapp and his friend Carl Malone were inspecting a yellow rubber life raft Jerry's father bought from an army and navy surplus store. Jerry told his friend it was a real navy survival raft. There was a huge pocket sewed on the side of it. They unzipped it and inside was canned goods, fishing equipment, a knife, and a large silver packet. They lifted the packet out. Printed on the side of it in bold letters were the following instructions. "PULL THE STRING AND DISPERSE CONTENTS ON THE WATER. IT WILL BE SEEN BY RESCUE AIRCRAFT." They looked at one another with real intensity. "Jerry I wonder what this stuff does when it gets in the water? I sure would like to know."

Jerry nodded his head. "I know how we can find out. Let's go to Riverside pool tonight when the guys sneak in after it closes and try it out."

"Yea, that's a great idea."

Later the guards at Riverside pool had cleared everyone out and locked the gates and doors. About ten boys hiding in the bushes close by were waiting for them to leave so they could sneak in and swim after hours. Most of them had been barred from the pool during open hours for breaking the rules. Regardless, this group of boys preferred swimming after the guards left. They could run, swear, dive, or anything they damned please and no one would bother them. The last car drove away from the parking lot which was located on top of the hill overlooking the pool. Someone shouted. "They're all gone, lets make it." Boys sprang from the bushes and ran to the fence. One of them grabbed the bottom of the chain link fence and pulled up. The others scrambled under it. Once the group was inside they put their legs against the fence and forced it up, so the boy who had been holding the fence outside could crawl in.

Clothes flew off as the boys ran to the water. No bathing suits for these guys. One of them yelled. "Bare Ass Beach is now open." They hit the water with running dives and cannon balls. They swore, shouted, and splashed each other in the face. Every rule of the big sign posted on the fence was broken.

Jerry and Carl could hear the shouting and laughing as they walked down the big hill to the pool. No one noticed them as they crawled under the fence with the big silver packet from the life raft. They jumped into the water and Jerry slowly pulled the string attached to the packet. A powdered substance immediately gushed out. Jerry was startled and he let go of it. As the big packet sunk to the bottom a dark cloud formed in the water around them and began to spread throughout the pool. Carl grabbed Jerry's arm and pulled him. "Let's get out of here." They quickly crawled under the fence and left.

The other boys continued to have fun, not noticing the change in the water. A couple of hours passed and it started to get dark. Ben Shinavare stared at the water. Something didn't look right. He shouted. "Hey, you guys, something is the matter with the water." No one paid attention. Complete darkness settled in. All activity in the pool stopped. The boys stared at one another and at the water in the pool. The pool was glowing an eerie green. Ben Shinavare shouted again. "I told you guys something funny was going on and you didn't listen."

Marty Gallager yelled back, "I don't know what the hell's happening. I'm getting out of here." He quickly climbed out of the pool. The other boys rushed to the side and scrambled out also. When they emerged from the water the green glowing stuff clung to their bodies like a cookie that had been dipped in chocolate frosting. They saw each other glowing in the dark. A frightened look came over their faces. They grabbed their clothes and lost no time getting under that fence. They ran up the hill bare naked glowing that eerie green.

The parking lot on top of the hill had turned into a lovers' lane as it did every night after it got dark. Cars were bumper to bumper. The group of naked bodies glowing the eerie green ran in between the cars to get as far away from the pool as possible. Loud screams erupted from the parked cars. Someone shouted, "They're coming from that bright thing below that hill." Car engines started up and tires squealed as they sped out of the park. The lovers lane cleared of every car.

The dispatcher sent two units. When they arrived at the pay phone where the complaint was called in, there were numerous couples waiting. Every one wanted to talk at once. The officers quieted them down shouting, "One at a time."

A man stepped forward. He pointed to the park. "Below that hill something must have landed. It's glowing like hell down there. These green creatures all lit up ran from whatever it is at the bottom of that hill. They were the weirdest looking things I ever saw. They were carrying some thing in their arms or what ever it was that was coming out of the sides of their bodies. The last time I saw them they ran across the street between those houses."

The officers looked confused. One of them asked, "Have you been drinking?"

The whole group came alive shouting. "We saw the damn things. Don't tell us we've been drinking. We were there."

The officers put up their arms. "Okay, we'll have a look. "Did anyone get hurt?"

Someone yelled. "No they didn't have a chance, we got the hell out of there too fast."

The officers drove over to the park. Sure enough there was a bright greenish glow coming from the bottom of the hill. They walked down and could see it was coming from the pool. They, too, crawled under the loose fence. One of the officers got a life-saving pole and pulled the packet from the water. He laughed when he read the bold letters on the side. "This packet contains luminescent chemicals. When they make contact with water they will glow brightly." They took the empty soggy container and went back to the crowd waiting at the pay phone. They showed them the empty packet and explained it was the cause of the glowing. The crowd still wasn't convinced. Someone shouted. "It's a cover up. They were aliens. I saw them."

BOB MORRISSEY

One Big Bite

The foundry was extra hot that night. Curtis wiped the sweat from his forehead and at the same time looked up at the large clock. He thought, it would only be an hour till lunch break. He reached down and tapped the brown paper bag that had his large pork chop sandwich inside. His mouth watered just thinking how good it was going to taste.

Time went by slowly on that hot monotonous job. He shook his head as he looked at the hot red liquid metal flowing past him in the large trough. He thought, man, this must be the worst job in the whole world. His thoughts got away from the job and went back to better things. Lunch hour, being outside in the cool air and that brown bag with the delicious pork chop sandwich inside.

The whistle finally blew for lunch break. The men grabbed their lunch pails and bags and ran for the door leading outside. Curtis had his lunch bag cradled in his arm like a half-back protecting the football.

The cool air outside felt good. He took a couple of deep breaths and went to the vending machine and got a can of soda. He made his way to a bench and straddled it. He put the brown paper bag down in front of him. He stared at it and thought eating lunch is the only good thing about

65

this job especially if you got a pork chop sandwich. He carefully tore the paper bag exposing his meal. In front of him was his prize that he had been dreaming about since he came to work, the big pork chop sandwich. He slowly picked up the sandwich with both hands. He stared at it thinking how good it was going to taste. He finally went to take a big bite when out of nowhere a large set of jaws with flashing white teeth exploded in front of him. The surprise knocked him off the bench. He immediately jumped up from the ground. He looked around and his pork chop sandwich was gone. The other workers were laughing and shouting.

"Over there, Curtis. That big dog snatched your sandwich."

Curtis looked and about twenty-five yards away stood a large black dog. His head was going up and down and his jaws were devouring the sandwich. Curtis shouted. "You mother ----- I'll break your damn neck." He grabbed a pipe and-rushed toward the dog cursing.

The dog saw him coming and the race was on. Curtis with a pipe in his hand and the dog with the pork chop sandwich in his mouth.

"Unit 12, this is the dispatcher. Go to the Erie Foundry parking lot. We have a disturbance. Man versus dog."

The Day It Rained Bloomers

It was 1963 and everything was in turmoil. The Flower people were in full bloom. Hippies smoking pot. Pressure groups active in their marches and riots. It seemed everyone wanted to be heard. This was a new chapter in police work. So many problems to deal with. In order to solve these matters someone had to gather information to know what was going on.

Two officers were picked to intermingle with these groups and find out what they were up to. They were instructed to dress and act like the people involved in the various organizations, and at no time let it be known they were police officers. The perfect men were chosen. Jim Pela known as Bug, and Mark Phiffer. Bug was a skinny little guy. The only reason he got his hair cut was as a police office he had to, now he could let it grow.

Mark Phiffer was a big easy going young man. Nothing seemed to excite him. He walked slow, talked in a low voice and never did any thing to draw attention.

A few weeks passed and Bug's hair was longer and in a pony tail. He tried to grow a mustache and beard but only got a few scraggly hairs under his nose and chin. Mark Phiffer grew a thick dark beard. Their vehicle was an old

Volkswagen Bus. They painted it a bright yellow and drew marijuana leaves on each side. Holes were punched in the muffler to make it loud.

They did an outstanding job. They picked up the hippie and dope dealers jargon. They played the part well. No one suspected they were police officers.

One night they were called on for a stakeout assignment. Some ladies who worked for the phone company had been attacked on four different occasions. They had been pulled into an alley, robbed and raped. A female officer was assigned to walk on the same sidewalks where the woman had been abducted. Bug was to dress like a street person and lay in a business doorway across the street as if he was spaced out on drugs and watch the decoy. His partner, Mark would stay in the van and observe through a one way mirror.

The officers were playing their roles. The lady officer in plainclothes was walking the sidewalk. Bug was laying across the street with his back propped against a door. Mark was in the van. Hours passed. Three young men approached the woman decoy. Bug leaned forward a little. The men saw the movement. One of them pointed at him. Bug sensed he might have spooked them. He pretended to stumble when he got on his feet. He staggered backwards and hugged the side of the building. He took a quick glimpse at the three men. One was pointing at him and the other ones were staring. He slowly unbuttoned his fly and urinated on the bay window of the business place. One of the men yelled,

"He's no cop. Cops don't piss on windows."

They grabbed the woman officer. Bug and Mark ran to her with their guns drawn. All three men were arrested. When the suspects were brought into the station they kept shouting. "Arrested by a jive-ass hippie who pisses on windows."

Everyone in the department except one guy thought the two men were doing a great job. Officer Harold Basil didn't like them because at night they used the daytime detectives' office to process the suspects they had arrested. Basil was a clean freak. When he came to work, the first thing he did was wipe off the keys to his typewriter with alcohol, then dust his desk and chair, grab his coffee cup that had been washed the day before and wash it again. He would then take a paper napkin and place it on his desk. Pour himself a cup of coffee, and put it on the napkin. Before taking a sip he would wash his hands.

Bug and Phiffer didn't worry about cleanliness. If they ate their lunches in the office they'd leave paper and crumbs on the desks. Bug smoked cigarettes. He let them dangle from his lip. He won't touch it with his hands. The ash would get extremely long. He never flicked it off. He waited till he couldn't get another puff off the cigarette then he'd put it out in his coffee. Without hesitation he'd drink the coffee - ashes and all.

On many occasions Bug and Phiffer would have to work over onto the day shift. Basil would watch Bug put his cigarette out in the coffee cup and drink it. He'd gag and yell, "You disgusting hog." Bug just smiled at him and put his coffee cup away without washing it. The next day he didn't wash it he just poured his coffee. The cup was originally white, but was now a stained brown.

Detective Basil had another problem with his working conditions. Over the years a lot of woman's bras and panties accumulated in a large box in the locker room next to the bathroom. These underclothes were taken for evidence in rape cases. After the cases went to court the evidence was thrown into the box. No one ever took the time to dispose of them. I guess since it was five floors down it seemed like too much work. Basil wanted to throw them out but the other detectives said some of those cases were still open and he better not. Of course they were kidding, but Basil didn't know.

One day Bug and Phiffer were working overtime doing their reports. The day shift detectives came to work. Right away Basil went through his ritual only this time he put on rubber gloves. After he was done wiping off his typewriter and dusting, he took out a can of disinfectant and begun spraying the office. Bug heard the whoshing sound over his head. He looked up to see the fine mist floating down on his head. He jumped to his feet and shouted. "If you ever do that again I'll shove that can so far up your ass you'll have to belch to get it out." Basil sprayed the can again. Bug went to swing but the other officers grabbed both him and Basil.

That night Bug brought a bag of fried chicken, and

French fries to the office. He took one of greasiest pieces of meat and rubbed it across the keyboard of Basil's typewriter. Small pieces dropped in between the keys. He wiped his hands on some paper towels and left them on top of the desk. He moistened a couple of kleenex and put them on his chair. He got Basil's coffee cup and removed the clean paper towel stuffed inside. He put some coffee in it then dropped a cigarette butt in. Bug then went into the rest room and poured water on the toilet seat. His partner, Phiffer stared at him. Bug shouted. "I'll fix that sissy. I ought a get him an apron. I'm going to get his ass, Phiffer."

Phiffer just stared. "Hey man, whatever turns you on."

Seven Forty Five in the morning. The day shift started to arrive. Detective Basil was the first. He walked to his desk and was horrified. "Who the hell was sitting at my desk? There's garbage all over it." He grabbed his cup and saw the cigarette butt floating in the stale coffee. He rubbed his fingers over the greasy keys to his typewriter then pointed to the used Kleenex and soiled paper towels.

"Some damn pig ate here and used my cup last night." He pointed to Bug. "Did you do this? You damn crud."

Bug got a serious look on his face. "Naw, I didn't do it. Last night we had a street person witness a shooting. We bought him a meal and gave him some coffee. He had a few sores on his mouth but other then that he was all right."

"You let the filthy bastard drink out of my cup?"

"Yea, it was the only one we could find."

Basil threw his cup against the wall shattering it. He

71

ran into the rest room to get his cleaning supplies. He shouted again. "Who the hell was using the toilet. There's piss all over the seat."

Phiffer laughed. "The street person was the last one in there."

Basil exploded into a rage shouting and kicking lockers. He grabbed the large box of bras and panties and ran to the window. He pitched them out. "I'm tired of this filthy place."

Meanwhile, five floors below on the steps was a militant group, protesting. The leader was on the top step with a bull horn shouting. "We'll burn the town down."

The panties filled with air and drifted down like miniature parachutes, landing very softly on the protesters.

A large stained bloomer dropped over the head of the leader.

He was startled and quickly tore it off. When he saw what had engulfed his head and face he slammed it to the ground and started spitting and cussing. The group was now staring up threatening with clenched fists. Needless to say there was a big investigation by Internal Affairs to why it rained bloomers that day. The case is still unsolved.

Unlucky Gambler

"Unit #11, 815 Washington St. apt. 10. Man shot, woman suspect still has gun and is firing. Make it a code three."

"Unit #11, okay." I reached to the dashboard and hit the overheads. My partner, Eddie, wrote down the address. The siren screamed, opening a path for us through the heavy traffic. I watched the numbers on the homes so I would not pull up in front of 815. I stopped two houses short.

If she was going to take a shot at us she'd have to shoot at an angle to hit us. We quickly got out of the car and ran through front yards. We felt relieved when we made it to the front porch. The glass window of the door was shattered. I assumed someone shot from the inside since all the broken glass was laying outside on the porch.

We entered the apartment house with guns drawn. We slid our backs against the wall with our guns aimed to the far end of the hall. Apartment 10 was the last one on the right. Eddie pointed at the chunks of plaster gouged out of the wall. He shaped his hand like a gun letting me know he thought they were made from bullets. I nodded.

We still were about 5 feet away from apartment 10

when the front door behind us opened. A woman shouted. "Some damn fool broke the window." It startled us and I started to turn around when the door to apartment 10 exploded open.

A heavy-set woman with a revolver in her hand shouting to the woman behind us. "You back for more bitch?"

Eddie and I yelled, "Drop it," and at the same time rushed her and grabbed the gun. Our momentum knocked her to the floor. We came down on top of her.

"Officers I ain't got no doings with you. I settled my problem with my old man. I'm looking for his bitch."

The three of us got up. I pointed to a chair. "Lady, you sit in that chair and don't get up. Now, tell us what happened?"

She pointed to a bedroom. "I was sleeping in my bed when that sap-sucker old man of mine came in with a bitch and turned on the light. He kicked the bed and yelled, 'Woman, I'm going to flip a quarter. If it comes out heads you stay. If it comes up tails you carry your sorry ass out of here and me and this broad stays.'

I got mad and pulled my gun from under the pillow and shot the fool. I tried to get the bitch but she ran."

Eddie with a serious look. "Where's your husband now?"

"He's in that bedroom."

We quickly drew our guns again and ran to the room. A motionless man was on the floor with a hole in his forehead. I dropped to my knees. Grabbed his wrist for a pulse. Found none.

Eddie picked up the man's clenched fist and unloosened his fingers. A quarter hit the floor and we both stared at it. It turned up heads. Eddie shook his head. "He lost twice." All indications were the man was dead. To be certain, we called an ambulance and had him transported to the hospital. The wife was taken to the police station.

When we went to the hospital for our follow up investigation, the doctor in the emergency room confirmed the man was D.O.A. (dead on arrival). Eddie put on rubber gloves and started to go into the man's pockets to collect his personal property for evidence and safe keeping. He jumped back and shouted, "Aw, man."

I ran to him. "What's the matter?"

His eyes were wide open. "When I was removing these dice from his pocket they fell. See what came up?"

I looked and the dots added up to seven. "So what's the problem?"

"He should have used the dice instead of that quarter. He'da been a winner."

BOB MORRISSEY

No Light Needed

Police officers see thousands of incidents as they pass through their careers. Most of them are soon forgotten, but a few stick in your memory forever. The story I'm about to tell you is one that I will never forget.

The story unfolded when I was handed a burglary investigation. It involved a forcible entry to a clothing store. I pulled up in front of Harry's Clothing Store. A man came running out the front door. "Officer, some no good broke into my store." I followed him through the store to the back room. The sun shone through a large hole in the ceiling. Shattered boards and ripped tar paper strewed the floor. The owner pointed to a pool of blood on the floor and a large sledge hammer near by. He shouted. "The damn fool must have slammed a hole in the roof and fell through. I wish he'd broke his thieving neck."

I agreed and bent over to examine the sledge hammer. I saw something under a cabinet. I reached under and found a leather wallet. I quickly opened it and pulled out the identification cards. Every one had the same name, "Anthony Harris." I looked at the owner. "He must have hit his head so hard his wallet flew out of his pocket. Does Anthony Harris work for you?"

77

"No, I never heard of the guy?"

"Well he was working last night in your store."

The owner laughed. "Yeah, I see what you mean."

I called two hospitals in the area hoping they treated a man whose name was on the I.D cards. Mercy Hospital said an Anthony Harris came in around three o'clock in the morning and was treated for a large laceration to his right arm. He also had a huge bump on his head. They told me the address he gave them and it jived with the addresses on the cards.

My blood tingled as I drove to Anthony Harris's home. I knocked on the door and a woman answered. I identified myself and asked if Anthony Harris lived there?

She nodded. "He's my son." She pointed to a stairway and said he was sleeping. I asked her if I could talk with him. She opened the door all the way and said, "Yes."

I climbed the steps and walked into a bedroom where a young man was sleeping. His right arm was above the covers and it was completely bandaged. The other arm was under the pillow. I quietly walked next to the bed and grabbed the arm that was under the pillow. I wanted to make sure there wasn't a gun in his hand. I slowly pulled his hand out and called his name.

He shook his head a couple of times and sat up.

I put my badge in front of his face. He shouted.

"Who's there?" I put my badge closer to his face. Again he yelled, "Who are you?"

I looked closer at the man and could not believe what I

saw. I was stunned. Both his eyes were frosted. How could this man be blind?

"Who are you? Answer me damn it."

"I'm a police officer."

The room went quiet. His head went upward and rocked side to side. "Well, you got me. I bet you have my wallet in your hand."

"Yes, Anthony, I have your wallet."

He got out of bed and felt for a chair where his clothes were. "Give me a couple of minutes till I get dressed. I'll go peacefully. There will be no trouble officer."

Driving to the police station I kept looking at the man. I still could not believe he was responsible for the break in. At the station I got us some coffee and rolls. We sat in the interrogation room facing each other. I didn't know what approach to use to start the questioning.

Anthony must have sensed I was having a problem. He sort of bowed his head and said. "I'll tell you how it happened."

He then gave this account of the incident. "In the afternoon I took a sledge hammer into the alley behind Harry's Clothing Store. I threw it on the roof of the store. I left the alley and came back after the store had closed. It was about two in the morning. I was not aware that someone must have seen me throw the sledge hammer on the roof earlier. Who ever it was climbed on the roof and smashed a hole in it. The fool must have been scared off and left the hammer on the roof. I crawled around on the roof till I found the sledge hammer. I stood up and raised it over my head and slammed it down with all my might. I was surprised when the heavy hammer didn't make contact with the roof. I was falling. I thought that I must of swung at the edge of the roof and was going to land in the alley. Instead I fell inside the store. I bounced off shelves and cabinets. I landed so hard on my head my wallet popped out of my back pocket."

Anthony hesitated and rubbed his head, "Man, that hurt like hell." He drank some coffee then continued. "I crawled all over that damn floor feeling for my wallet but couldn't find it. My arm was bleeding real hard so I found my way to the back door and unlocked it. I knew I would get caught because someone would find my wallet."

I sat there spellbound. I didn't know what to say. Anthony again spoke. "Officer, you've been pretty good to me; I want to tell you more. I broke into twelve more stores." He went into detail how he did each one.

I checked with the record bureau and they had a crime report for each one of them. I asked Anthony, "Doesn't being blind cause a real handicap for you when you break into buildings?"

"No, I have the advantage over a person with sight. When I break into a dark building I don't need a flashlight. If a person has a light on the police can see it from the outside. I can walk the streets at any hour of the night and people or police don't suspect me of anything. A few nights ago I left stores I had broken into and was walking home with my cane. The police saw me walking and drove me home because they felt sorry for me."

I looked at Anthony and told him I too felt sorry this had happened, but there was nothing I could do for him at this time. He would have to go to court for what he had done.

"Don't worry officer, I understand. It won't be all that bad. The pen will assign a con to me and he'll be my seeing eye dog. Maybe the pen will be better than the outside."

The case was heard before Judge Macelwane and she found Anthony guilty. The judge commented that of all the cases she had heard, she had never experienced one like this.

BOB MORRISSEY

The Big Mistake

Marty's was different. The clientele was like oil and water, but this mixture worked. One group was made up of excons, burglars, robbers and every other type of low life. The other group were tough cops who liked to have a drink without someone bothering them. Both groups kept their occupations to themselves. When you entered the bar you were met by a large sign that said, NO MOTHER TALK.

The Chief of Police and Internal Affairs, were constantly trying to monitor what was happening in Marty's. They became frustrated. No one would ever squeal.

Marty, the owner, was a short stocky guy with a nose flattened from past fights. Many times he had been brought in and questioned about ruckuses that were supposed to have happened in his bar. Each time he had the right answers.

One of the older officers, Deputy Chief Morgan, would occasionally stick up for the bar. He made the statement once, "Marty's is the greatest training place in the world. You don't learn about criminals in Sunday school." Of course he got some strange looks from the chief, and Internal Affairs officers. He defended himself after interpreting these stares. "Many times we have solved important cases from our officers who hung out in Marty's. The criminals in there trusted our men and gave them valuable information."

On occasion I went into Marty's. They didn't need paid entertainment. Something strange and exciting was always happening. There were so many fights no one bothered to turn around when one erupted.

The women who frequented the place were free spirited... really free spirited. When you ordered a drink the bartender would ask, "A glass with lipstick, or one that has been washed?"

Marty liked to open beer bottles with his belly button. He thought it was the greatest trick. If someone complained he'd laugh, "I'll give you a free one if there's lint on it."

One night the big mistake happened. Three out of town hoods cruised the streets of Toledo looking for a place to rob. On Main Street they saw Marty's place all lit up. The driver said, "That's the joint, lot of customers and look at all the cars. The cash register must be full. Let's take it down."

They parked a half-block away in a dark area and checked out their shotguns, then concealed them under their long overcoats.

Entering Marty's they boldly walked the length of the bar, staring and studying the many customers. The off-duty cops, and ex-cons were street wise. They knew what was about to come down.

The three out of town robbers suddenly threw open

their overcoats and produced their shotguns. For effect, they quickly pulled down the slides of their shotguns, seeding shells in the chambers. This action made a loud clanging sound. Everyone in the bar was familiar with that noise. The crowd became silent. All eyes were on the three men with the long overcoats and shotguns.

Two robbers pointed their guns at the customers. The other one aimed his at the barmaid. They shouted, "This is a hold up. Everyone of you slime balls hit the floor. All we want to see is asses and elbows."

The barmaid made no attempt to go to the cash register. She plugged her ears with her fingers and dove under the bar. No one else followed the orders. Instead an eruption of gunfire and loud cursing ensued. The war was on.

The next day a Canadian radio station C.K.L.W. reported it best. "Last night in Toledo, Ohio, three armed bandits tried to rob a local watering hole for off-duty policemen. When the smoke cleared, two robbers were on the slab and the other one was in the slammer."

Homicide and Internal Affairs detectives handled the investigation. They confiscated the guns of the officers who were in Marty's when the robbery went down. The doctors from St. Vincent's Hospital turned over thirty nine bullets taken from the robbers bodies. Ballistic and other tests determined that thirty projectiles came from officers guns. The remaining nine slugs taken from the robbers' bodies are still a mystery.

To the street - wise cops who hang out in Marty's, it's

no mystery where those other nine shots came from. No one will ever know because they don't squeal.

"By the way, Marty's has never been robbed since the big mistake."

Showers On Clear Days

Three boys about eleven or twelve years old were sitting on the curb. A fourth was kicking a can in the street. They were bored and kept asking one another what they wanted to do. Carl, the one kicking the can, shouted, "I'll show you how to have some fun but you got to be able to run fast." The three boys sitting on the curb looked up at him.

"First of all we go over to that drinking fountain and drink as much water as your stomach can hold. Then follow me to the bridge. I guarantee we'll have fun."

The boys didn't question Carl. Whatever he had in mind was better then sitting on the curb. They went to the fountain and drank as much as they could. Carl encouraged them to drink more. "In order for this to work, you have to carry as much water as you can." The boys felt like their stomachs were bursting as they walked behind Carl to the bridge.

On top of the bridge the boys were doing a dance trying to hold all the water they drank. Mike had a painful expression on his face. He shouted. "Carl, where is the restroom?"

Carl instructed them. "Unbutton your barn doors and

lean up against that railing. Let it go on those guys down there working on the tugs. Mike was dancing and shaking his head. "I don't know about doing that. Those tuggers are pretty big and they're mean."

Carl shouted back. "You wanted to have fun didn't you? Those guys will chase us if we get them mad. We're faster then they are. By the time they get up here we'll be gone. You see that marsh on the other side of the river? We'll run there and hide in the bushes"

Meanwhile, below the bridge, the crew of the tug was sitting on the deck. They were in front of the boat in the shadow of the bridge. Their lunches were spread out on a bulkhead and they were enjoying their meals and the nice breeze coming from the river. Harry, who had been below deck working on the engine, had his shirt off. He was a stocky man with dark hair covering his chest and back. His large arms were covered with tattoos. He was first to react. He jumped up and quickly rubbed the back of his head and chest. He shouted. "Where in the hell is that water coming from?"

A couple of other crewmen slapped at their heads. One of them yelled. "Is it raining? I don't see how it could. It's a clear day."

Another man who was looking up at the bridge laughed, "It's not raining. Those punks up there are pissing on your heads."

Harry, who was wiping the back of his head, looked up and saw the boys leaning against the railing laughing at him. He shouted. "You little bastards. If I get hold of you, I'll pull that thing out by the roots."

This was what the boys wanted. They made obscene gestures with their fingers and shouted remarks questioning Harry's manhood. The men jumped to the dock and ran to the steps leading to the top of the bridge, cussing all the way. The boy's young legs sprang into a dash to the other side of the bridge.

They ran into the marsh and hid in some underbrush. Carl whispered. "Quit laughing. If those guys catch us they'll kick our ass."

The boys continued to hide for about fifteen minutes. Carl's head slowly raised to the top of the weeds. He looked across the river and saw the men working on the tug again. "It's all clear. Let's walk down to the other bridge to make sure they don't see us."

Days went by, and whenever the boys were bored and needed some excitement one of them would say. "Hey you guys, lets go water the tuggers." It worked every time. The tuggers would always chase them, but could never catch them. The boys had the advantage since the tuggers didn't know what time they would appear above them.

One day the boys' luck ran out. They climbed into the understructure of the bridge and were catching pigeons. They were concentrating so hard catching the birds they didn't see the large freighter headed for the bridge. All at once, the bridge started to lift to let the boat through. The boys hugged the metal girders and went up with the span.

The bridge tender saw the boys hanging on for all they're worth. He called the police.

The first crew arrived. One officer grabbed a coil of rope and climbed to where the boys were. The other officer ran to the tug docks. The officer shouted to Harry telling him what was going on. They jumped on the tug and threw the tie ropes onto the dock. Harry maneuvered the tug close to the bridge so in the event the boys or the officer fell they could reach them fast.

The officer who climbed up to the boys secured them with the rope. He motioned the bridge tender to bring the span down.

Harry was watching through his field glasses. He quickly put them down and cupped his hands around his mouth. He shouted up at the officer with the boys. "Hey, hold them punks. We've been trying to catch them for a couple of months."

The boys were placed in the back of the paddy wagon. The crew of the tug gathered behind, staring into the open doors. The boys' heads were all bowed. One of the men who had been rained-on took out a large knife from a sheath he was wearing. "Officers just let me have five minutes with them and I guarantee they won't have a nozzle to shower anyone again."

The officers looked at the boys. "Well what do you have to say to these men? They helped save your lives." The boys looked fearfully at the men. They apologized. The officers took them home to their parents. They explained what had been happening for the past couple of months. The parents had very concerned looks. They assured the officers there would be no more showers on clear days.

BOB MORRISSEY

He Stapled His Wig On

Let your eyebrows grow and comb them back. What do you comb your hair with, a washrag? You got enough bare head for two faces. These thoughts were constantly running through Carl's mind. One day he walked past a small shop and noticed toupees displayed in the window. He stared at them and imagined how he would look with one. He thought maybe if he wore a wig it would put a stop to all the wise remarks the guys make at work.

He walked in and was met by a small thin man with a pencil line mustache. "Can I help you sir?"

Carl pointed to his bald head. "You got something to cover it up?"

"I'm sure we do." He directed Carl to a table with a large mirror attached. Carl kept looking over his shoulder to see if anyone he knew came in. He quickly sat down. The salesman stared at Carl's head and mumbled to himself then went to the back room. When he returned he was petting a furry little thing as if it was a pet. He walked behind Carl and dropped it on his head. Carl was startled and jumped from the chair. "Don't worry it won't bite." The salesman patted Carl's back and eased him back down in the chair.

93

Again he placed the hair piece on Carl's head. Carl could not believe how different he looked. He shouted "I'll take it."

"Shall I wrap it up?"

"Hell no, leave it right where it is."

As he walked home Carl smiled at his reflection in every store window he passed. It sure was different seeing that hair on top of his head. He felt like a new man. He thought, I'll bet this will put a stop to the wise remarks the guys at work make about me. No more chrome dome, or skin head.

That night he slept with the wig on. In the morning he was careful when he passed the comb through it. Driving to work he kept anticipating what the guys were going to say.

He slowly opened the door to the shop and walked on his tip toes down the hall to the coffee room where the guys congregated before work. He stood in the doorway and no one recognized him. He shouted. "Good morning." Everyone stared with squinted eyes.

Charlie Mapp pointed and laughed. "If it isn't topper. Look who got himself a rug." The men got up from the table and crowded around Carl trying to put their hands on his wig.

"Don't touch. This cost a lot of money. Keep your damn hands off it. I don't want any bullshit."

Charlie Mapp shook his head. "We wouldn't do anything like that Carl. You really look good with that fur on your head."

"Knock off the crap Charley. I saw you wink to those guys."

"No, believe me. It really does something for you. I don't know what. But it does something for you. How do you make it stay on your head?"

"Well they gave me a tube of glue. I squeeze it on my scalp and I push the wig down on it."

"You mean to say that the only thing that keeps that on your head is glue?"

"Yeah, but I got to watch out, when the wind blows, it feels like it's going to fly off."

"They didn't tell you what to do when you go out in the wind?"

"No, were they supposed to?"

"Well, you got to staple it on."

"Staple it on? Man, that would hurt like hell."

"Naw, your head is made out of bone. Everyone knows there aren't any nerves in bone. All the guys with wigs staple them on when they go out in the wind. If they didn't wigs would be sailing around like flying squirrels. Isn't that right you guys?"

The men all nodded. Some of them said. "He's right Carl. You don't want that thing to blow away."

"That's strange. That guy should have told me."

Everyone went to work. The only noise was the humming of the machinery. A few hours passed and some-one shouted, "Lunch time. Let's go get some hot dogs." The machines were shut down and the men rushed into the washroom.

Carl sneaked into the office. He slowly picked up the stapler. All the men in the washroom stood straight up when they heard the piercing painful scream. "You dirty rotten lying sons of bitches." The men laughed until Carl appeared with a wild look, screaming and wielding a pipe wrench. "I'll kill everyone of you no good bastards." Frightened men were now running out doors and climbing through the windows.

"Unit #2. Go to the Front Street Machine Shop. Better step it up. There's a demented man with a pipe wrench."

The officers arrived and Carl was being held down by four men. He was cursing and threatening and trying to break loose. The officers calmed him down and lifted him to his feet. Carl was explaining what happened when he got mad again and threw his wig to the floor and kicked it like a football. He pointed to the men. "I'll get even with every-one of you clowns."

Chuckie Can't Handle His Liquor

At a local tavern by the river men, were sitting around drinking and exchanging fish stories, some true and some false. The front door opened and an old guy walked in. One could tell he was a outdoors man from his clothing and weather beaten face. He carried a large woodchuck under his arm. Everybody stepped aside as they stared at the big animal when it passed. The old guy pulled a stool away from the bar with his foot and sat down. He dropped the woodchuck on the bar and it immediately sat erect with his paws drawn to its chest.

The bartender cautiously walked to the old man. "That thing bite?"

"Hell, no. Chuckie here has been my pet for years."

"Well, what you want to drink, Pop?"

"Give me a double shot of whiskey and a beer wash."

The bartender nodded his head and in a short time returned with the drinks. He cautiously put the glasses down while all the time staring at the sitting woodchuck. The old guy grabbed the shot glass raised it to his mouth then suddenly put it back on the bar. "Sorry, Chuckie, I forgot about you." He petted the animal's head, picked up a half dollar and threw it to the bartender. "Give me some peanuts for Chuckie." The bartender caught the coin, and took a packet of nuts from a rack and slid it to him.

The Old guy ripped the top off the cellophane bag with his teeth, and took out a large nut. The woodchuck's paws were outstretched begging. The old guy gave him the large nut. The animal took it in his paws and immediately nibbled it.

The bartender stood in disbelief. He was reluctant to let the woodchuck stay, but he saw all the men gathered around it. He felt this was good for business and he decided to let it remain. One guy shook his head. "Man, I never saw anything like this. That thing is almost human." He tapped the old gent on the shoulder. "Hey, Pop, where did you get that thing?"

The old timer slowly spun around on the stool. "Well you see boys, I'm a trapper from up Erie, Michigan way. One cold wet morning I saw this young woodchuck on the road hugging his dead mother. She must had been killed by a car. I tried to help her but she was a goner. The little guy stared at me with his big eyes. I could swear he was crying. I took the little orphan home and hand fed him till I thought he was old enough to make it on his own. I set him loose but he would not go. He kept coming back crying. He was a lonesome critter and needed a friend. I looked at his pitiful face and thought of his dead mother. I had no choice but to take in the little guy. He has been a grateful friend ever since."

The barroom became silent. The old man looked at the

sorry expressions on the men's faces. He felt he had them where he wanted them. The free drinks and peanuts were stacking up in front of him and his woodchuck.

One of the group yelled. "Hey old timer, Chuckie has been eating a lot of salty peanuts. He ought'a have some thing to drink to wash them down."

The sly old guy raised his empty glasses. "Yeah, I believe Chuckie and I could use a drink. Give me a whiskey with a beer wash. Get Chuckie a blackberry brandy and put it in a soup bowl."

The bartender looked at the animal suspiciously. "Hey, I don't know about serving a woodchuck."

Men held up money and shouted. "Hell he's old enough. You served him nuts, why not a drink?"

The bartender saw all the money being flashed in front of him. He shouted, "Why not." He got a bowl from the kitchen and poured a shot of blackberry brandy into it.

The men shouted, "More, make it half full. Chuckie's thirsty." The bartender hesitated looked at the money and poured till the bowl was half full. He placed the drinks in front of the old timer. The old guy slid the bowl in front of the woodchuck. Chuckie didn't hesitate. His head dove into the bowl and lapped up the blackberry brandy.

Everyone laughed and cheered Chuckie on.

Someone yelled, "That damn woodchuck drinks like an alcoholic friend of mine. The guy shakes so bad in the morning he has to drink out of a soup bowl too. If he drank from a glass it would splatter all over him. After he gets the first one down he's as steady as a surgeon. Wait till I see him drinking like that again. I'm going to call him Chuckie."

The men got braver. Some stood next to the woodchuck. A few petted it. A man who sat next to the old man looked at his friend. "I don't know about you but I'm moving. Every time that damn thing drinks he looks a little wilder. If it was tame when it came in here, that stuff he's drinking is going to make him untame."

His friend laughed. "There's nothing to worry about. Old Chuckie is one of the boys. Stick around."

"You stick around, I'm going to that table by the door. When he goes crazy, I'm out of here."

He no sooner said it when a painful scream pierced the room followed by glasses and chairs being overturned. "The bastard bit me. The damn thing can't hold his liquor. He wants to fight." Men scattered from the bar. The old man continued to drink. Chuckie ran up and down the bar showing his teeth and hissing. His fur was bristled.

Someone yelled."Better get the hell out of his way. Those things have a nasty bite." The woodchuck dove to the floor and under the tables. Everyone pointed to where they thought he was. Chuckie bounced off table legs and walls.

The bartender ran to the old man who had his head on the bar and was sleeping. He reached over and shook his shoulders. "Hey, you, wake up and get that woodchuck the hell out of here."

His head came up from the bar and wobbled. In a slurred voice he said."One thing I learned a long time ago. Don't mess with Chuckie when he's drinking." His head dropped to the bar and he went back to sleep.

A brave drunk grabbed a tablecloth and stretched it out in front of him. He staggered and slurred. "Where's the damn thing? I'll wrap him up and throw him out the door." He made his way to the woodchuck. His head wobbled and his eyes were squinted. "I thought there was only one." He threw the tablecloth and Chuckie caught it with his teeth. He spun around and shredded it to pieces.

The bartender tried to wake the old man again. It was no use. He ran to the phone and called the police. "Please send me some help. A drunken woodchuck is tearing up my bar. No, I have not been drinking."

Two officers entered the bar and saw several men standing on tables. The bartender had his finger over his lips motioning the officers to be quiet. He pointed to a stool where the old man was sleeping with his head on the bar. Below him was a woodchuck napping. The bartender whispered. "Please officers, don't wake that damn thing." One officer left the bar and came back with a dog catching pole. The other got an empty beer case.

The noose of the pole was eased over the woodchuck's neck and his limp body was lowered into the beer case. The officer with the pole looked at the bartender.

"You didn't have to worry about him waking up he's stoned."A sober customer drove the old man and his pet home. As the officers left the bar, one smiled, "I wonder if Chuckie will have a hangover tomorrow?"

Two Minute Moe

After roll call Sergeant Hinkle called a meeting of all the officers who walked beats.

"Listen men, we got burglars raising havoc with the stores in the business district. Pay as much attention as you can to the rear of these buildings. Check every door to see if it is locked. Shine your flashlights on the windows. Remember, if you don't see a reflection coming off the window someone must have broken it and taken out the remaining fragments. Let's check those alleys for anything that looks suspicious. Make sure you got fresh batteries in your flash lights. A bright light is as important as your gun. Let's see if we can round up whoever is responsible for these burglaries."

I checked out my equipment and got new batteries for my light. I shined it in the eyes of other officers and they shielded their eyes and cussed. Seeing their reaction I knew the light was bright.

I made one complete tour of my beat, checking windows and doors. It was now two thirty in the morning. All the people and cars had vanished from the streets. I felt I had the whole area to myself, then I thought back to what Sergeant Hinkle had said. Those burglars could be working

103

on your beat.

I entered the alley behind Laselles, a large clothing store. It was pitch black. I waited till my eyes adjusted and walked as close to the buildings as possible so my body wasn't silhouetted by the lights coming from the street behind me. About a quarter of the way in, I noticed a car parked facing me behind the store. I squinted and stared at it. I positioned myself so the light from the far end of the alley was behind the rear window of the car.

Every once in a while a profiled head would bob up and then go back down. It would not be wise to approach the front of this car so I exited the alley the way I came in and walked to the other entrance. Again my eyes adjusted to the darkness. I hugged the building and approached the rear of the car. I thought to myself, gotta be forceful and take command when I confront that lookout man. The element of surprise was on my side and I must say the right thing. I decided to shout, get your hands up where I can see them you son of a bitch.

I eased up to the side of the car and slid my revolver out of the holster. I held the flashlight in my other hand. I tried to look in the windows but they were so fogged up I couldn't see anything.

I jerked the door open and flashed the light inside yelling, "Put your hands where I can see them, you son of a bitch." Suddenly my body froze and my eyes came wide open. Instead of a lookout in the car, there was a man and a woman, nude, all tangled up making love.

HUMOROUS BEAT

The man shouted. "Ah, man, give me two minute moe."

BOB MORRISSEY

Never Should Of Retired

One month after he retired, Lefty Henzler knew that he had made a mistake. Every minute without let up his wife complained about something. In order to get away from her he went to the neighborhood bar every morning. The guys who hung around in there were almost as annoying. Some complained about everything. Others told the same corny jokes over and over. Some got so drunk they didn't make sense. He always sat next to the ones who got stoned. He only had to say, "Is that right" when they tried to carry on goofy conversations with him.

The bar scene was getting tiresome, but he thought it was better then being nagged by his wife. One day his wife came in the bar and made a scene. She was angry because he never came home. He agreed with her and went home and had a talk. Martha told him to act like other men. Take care of the grass and plants get some shrubs and make their yard look good.

Lefty was not a lawn man. He hated cutting grass and pulling weeds. But he would do it to keep her quiet. He went to the garden store and bought flowers, sod, and fertilizers. It was the middle of summer and it was hot. Lefty worked two straight days in that heat making his yard

107

perfect. He cussed all the time. He got a beer and sat on the front step and wiped the sweat from his brow. *I should have stayed at the shipyards riveting. It was hard work but it was fun working with tough, crazy, guys.* It brought a smile to his face. He came back to reality and stared at the fresh-cut lawn and the new bushes. It looked good but this was not his bag. He shook his head. *Is this all I have to look forward to?*

As he cussed under his breath three teen aged boys walked over his lawn. One had a blaring radio on his shoulder. The other two strutted with the music. Lefty didn't say anything. He just stared at them. They dropped two empty soda bottles and flipped cigarette butts on his lawn.

Lefty jumped to his feet. "Hey, numb-nuts, pick up those bottles." The boys ignored him and one stuck up his middle finger.

Lefty ran in front of them with a shovel. "You better hear me screw heads. Pick up those bottles or I'll break this shovel on you."

A scout car was patrolling and the officers saw the ruckus. They got out of the car and calmed the situation. The boys picked up the bottles and cigarette butts from the lawn. Lefty's wife heard the commotion and ran from the house.

She grabbed Lefty by the arm and pulled him to the porch. "I can't leave you alone for a minute. You're driving me crazy. I don't know what you're going to do next. Why don't you get a job? Better yet I'll get you one."

Lefty shrugged his shoulders grabbed his beer and sat back on the step. Two days later Martha informed Lefty that her friend's husband owned a stretch limousine business and he needed drivers. She told her friend that Lefty would be interested.

Lefty squinted. "A chauffeur, that's not my bag."

Marth looked irritated. Lefty knew that look and that there wouldn't be any peace for a week. "Oh, okay I'll give it a try."

Lefty got the job and was handed a tuxedo and a black hat with a patent leather bill. He didn't like wearing this uniform, but he would do it for his wife. He put it on and mumbled, "Anything to keep her quiet." He stared at the long black car. *Why in the hell does it have to be so long?* He looked inside. It was plush. The seats were covered with soft leather. A complete bar faced the back seat. Lefty was still looking the car over when a couple about thirty years old walked up. They both had drinks in their hands and were half stoned.

"You the guy who is going to chauffeur us?"

Lefty nodded. "I guess so, I'm the only one here."

The guy shouted. "Well open the damn door. We want to get it on." Lefty stared at him and slowly opened the door.

Lefty didn't like the guy but he managed to calm himself. "Where do you want to go?"

"Listen Bozo, just drive and I'll tell you after we get

going. Get back here and dust off the seats."

Lefty ignored him and got in behind the steering wheel. The engine roared. Lefty was angry and pushed hard on the gas pedal. The guy in the back seat shouted something but he was drowned out by the squealing of the tires. Once on the road Lefty again asked. "Where do you want to go?"

The guy shouted. "I told you to drive. Just keep driving. When I feel like telling you where we want to go, I'll tell you. Meanwhile just drive and don't bother us."

Lefty could feel the sweat running down his back. The hair on the back of his neck was bristling. He kept saying to himself, *I got to keep calm.* A half hour passed and the couple was doing a lot of drinking and laughing. Every time Lefty would hear something coming from the back seat he'd look in the rear view mirror. The guy would shout,"Hey jerk quit looking back here. Just drive, don't look."

An hour passed and Lefty was about to ask for the destination again. He looked in the rearview mirror and saw the couple had their clothes off and were all tangled up. He kept driving. *No wonder he didn't tell me where to go. I got to keep my cool. I got to keep my cool. No way am I going to get mad.* He smiled and drove to the down town district where there was a lot of traffic and people crossing the streets. He made it a point to stop at every crosswalk where the people were waiting to cross. The couple in back didn't pay any attention to the people who looked in. They continued doing what they were doing. When they got done the guy shouted. "Hey slope head, stop the car and get back here and pour our champagne."

That did it. Lefty brought the car to a screeching stop. He jumped out and jerked the back door open. "You want champagne, you son of a bitch." He grabbed the champagne from the ice bucket and popped the cork hitting the guy in the head with it. He put his thumb over the open mouth of the bottle and shook it then squirted the nude couple. They screamed. Their hands flew up trying to protect their naked bodies from the cold liquid. When that bottle emptied, Lefty grabbed another one and continued squirting and cussing. Lefty gripped the bottle by the neck, and with a mean look shouted, "Now you two get the hell out of this car or I'll break this over your perverted heads." He started leaning in and the frightened couple jumped out the other door. Lefty drove off. He smiled when he saw them both standing at the curb, bending over with their hands covering their privates. He drove back to the office and parked the car. He threw the keys on the boss's desk. "I quit. I'm out of here."

"Martha saw him coming up the side walk. She came out on the front porch. "Well how did your first day on the job go?"

He shook his head.. "Just get me a beer.. I'm going to sit on this porch and drink till the cops come."

BOB MORRISSEY

Liquor Agents

Danny Murry was driving home from the wedding reception and thought he'd have a nightcap before going to bed. He saw a lighted bar with about twenty five motorcycles parked out front. This place looked like there was a lot of action going on inside. He parked next to the cycles and went in. He sat at the bar which was shaped like a big horse shoe and it didn't take him long to determine this was a rough place. The people were dressed in their colors. And the words they were using could not be found in the dictionary. He thought it would be wise to leave, but his curiosity wouldn't let him.

The dancers gyrated to the loud music. One guy had a lit cigarette jammed between his ear and his head, this gave him the freedom to use his hands however he wanted on his dance partner. A pack of cigarettes was rolled up in his tee shirt sleeve on his shoulder. Another guy danced with his motorcycle helmet on. Danny enjoyed this. It was better then a floor show.

The guy with the motorcycle helmet came back to the bar and sat directly across from Danny. Danny stared at him waiting for him to take off the helmet. The guy never did. He shouted at Danny, "Hey dip shit, what you looking at?"

Danny grinned."Not much."

"A wise ass, huh." He got up and so did a few other men sitting next to him. They walked to where Danny was sitting. They didn't say anything just started punching. Danny tried to defend himself but there were too many of them. He was slammed to the floor, and they kicked him. The bouncers came running and grabbed Danny's unconscious body and threw it into the alley.

Danny came to and he wiped the blood from his face. He got to his feet and walked to his car, hunched over and holding his ribs. He looked at the bar as he drove off and thought, this isn't over.

The next day his friends saw him. After he explained what happened, they all wanted to go to the bar and get even for what happened to their friend. Danny assured them this was not the best thing to do right now. He had a plan and would tell them when they should execute it. One month passed. Danny went into the pool room and asked his friends if they still wanted to help him. Everyone nodded and shouted, "let's go."

Danny held up his hands. "Now wait a minute. I've got a plan. Here's what I want you to do, put on suits and we'll go to the bar."

Someone shouted. "Put on my good clothes to fight some jerk. Man, I only got one suit. And I don't want it tore up."

"Now listen you guys, just let me tell you the whole thing. If we do this right we won't have to throw a punch." He explained the rest of the plan.

114

That night at one thirty in the morning they showed up at the bar dressed in suits. As usual there were a lot of motorcycles parked out front. They walked in and sat down. They didn't pay attention to the strange stares they got from the waitresses and customers. Danny and his friends ordered their drinks. Danny nodded his head and a couple of his friends got up and walked around the inside making it obvious they were studying the layout of the place.

One of the waitresses went to the office in the rear of the bar. In a short time, a man came out with a concerned look on his face. He brought a case of beer to one of the coolers which was close to where Danny and his friends were sitting. Danny knew the man was trying to hear the conversation he was having with his friends. He cupped his hands and in a low voice said. "The clock is ten minutes fast. When that clock says two twenty we grab the drinks on the bar and tables and take this place down."

The guy who was filling the cooler quickly left. A half case of beer remained on the floor. He went to all his waitresses and bartenders. "We got liquor agents in here. At five after two I want every drink picked up. No more drinks will be served after two o'clock." One of the bartenders shook his head.

"But boss, the law says we don't have to pick up the drinks till two thirty."

"I said drinks stop being served at two o'clock. Five after two all drinks will be picked up. Do you understand?" They all nodded.

When the clock struck two Danny and his friends got up and walked to different parts of the bar and stared at the clock on the wall then to their wrist watches. The boss shouted, "Pick them up." The bartenders grabbed all the drinks on the bar. The waitresses quickly cleared the tables. Loud shouts were erupting.

"Put my damn drink back. What the hell is going on. I paid for that drink. You better put it back. I got till two thirty."

The boss shouted to his bouncers. "Clear the place." The bouncers grabbed their clubs and tried to move the bikers out.

The bikers would have nothing to do with this. They were shouting, "Give us our drinks back or we'll tear up the place." This was the spark that erupted the explosion. Chairs were now flying at the bouncers. Glasses and beer bottles were breaking. Danny and his friends maneuvered to the exits and went to their cars. They laughed when two men came crashing out the big front window. In a short time the police cars with red lights flashing and sirens screaming pulled up.

It took about ten minutes to put the fight down. A single line of handcuffed men were brought out. Danny saw the guy who was wearing the helmet the night he was worked over. As he was pushed into the paddy wagon he was screaming and cussing that he wanted his money back. Danny walked up to the officers who were standing at the back of the wagon. He pointed inside at the guy who had been wearing the helmet. "Officers, I am a good citizen of this community. I don't condone this type of conduct. That man right there started the whole thing. He is a barbarian and I will testify against him."

The big guy stared at Danny and struggled to get free. "Man, what the hell you putting the mouth on me? If I get loose, I'll kill you."

"See, officer, what I mean. The man is not civilized. He needs to serve time. He started this ruckus. I want to testify in court against him."

The handcuffed motorcyclist dove head first cussing and threatening Danny. The officers caught him as he was flying out of the paddy wagon. They pushed him back in and slammed the doors. They told Danny to leave and they would get in touch with him if they needed him.

Two weeks later Danny read in the paper. "Motorcyclists given stiff fines and jail time for tavern ruckus." He nodded his head and smiled.

BOB MORRISSEY

Proved A Lot To Me

The neighborhood boys, as usual, were playing basketball in the vacant lot. Across the street another boy picked up a piece of roofing shingle and sailed it into the air. It flew in a straight line then turned and nose-dived into the group. The game stopped immediately. One boy dropped to his knees holding his hands over his eyes. Blood was streaming between his fingers and running down his wrists and forearms. A youth broke from the group screaming and ran to the nearest home for help.

In a short time a scout car pulled up. Two officers ran to the injured youth. One officer knelt next to the boy. The other opened the first aid kit. The officer kneeling next to the boy talked softly and patted him on the back.

"We're police officers son we're going to help you." He grabbed the boy's wrists and slowly pulled them away from his face. A large gash, bleeding profusely, was where his eye once was. The officer cringed and turned away- "Were not waiting for the ambulance. We'll transport." His partner ripped the wrapper off a large bandage and quickly placed it over the wound.

"Hold this on your eye son. I'm going to pick you up and carry you to the scout car." The other officer grabbed the emergency kit ran to the car and slid behind the wheel. His partner rushed with the boy and placed him on the back seat. As soon as he got in beside the boy he shouted.

"Hit it."

Tires squealed, and the siren wailed. The boys ran to the curb and watched the squad car speed away with their friend.

From the day of that terrible accident Billy Thomas's life has been in the dark. The doctors tried to save his sight with numerous operations but none were successful.

Billy was only twelve years old at the time of the accident and already excelled in sports. Every high school coach in the city hoped Billy would attend his school.

Years passed, Billy never gave up. Every time a doctor said there was a new type of operation that might get his sight back, he'd have it done, only to have the doctors say, "Sorry Billy, we tried." After the last operation it was decided Billy would never see again. Billy went to special schools to help him cope with being blind. He received a seeing eye dog, a large German Shepherd that he named Spike. He never complained and never talked about the accident, or how good he would have been in sports. He knew his life was restricted and he was going to make the best of it. His friends never forgot him. They came to his home every day.

Billy called his friend Harry Morgan one day and asked him if he would take him for a ride. Harry dropped every thing he was doing and came and got Billy. They were driving around and Harry asked. "Well what's been going on Billy?"

"Oh nothing. Harry, would you do me a big favor?"

"Sure, name it."

"I'd like to go to the Topsy-Turvy Bar and have a couple of beers."

"Why the Topsy-Turvy Bar? That's the meanest bar in town. It's on the east side. Those guys over there hate us. If they catch us in their bar they'll knock the hell out of us. Let's go to one of our neighborhood bars like the Bide Away."

"I've been thinking a lot lately. I really want to go there. I don't think there'll be a problem. Besides Harry, you're good with your fists."

"Sure, I can handle myself but I'll be outnumbered over there. Those guys will gang up on me."

"You don't want to take me there because I'm blind. I understand. Forget it. Will you take me home?"

Harry didn't know what to say. He looked over at his friend with his head bowed and the dark glasses on.

"Okay, I'll take you to the Topsy-Turvy."

The Topsy-Turvy Bar was near the ship docks and the foundries. It was a older building that needed a paint job. The windows had been covered over so people couldn't see inside.

"Well, we're here. I want to tell you this place is a dump." Harry grabbed Billy by the elbow and was going to help him out of the car.

"No, don't help me. Please let me do it myself." Billy got out of the car and called Spike who jumped out and stood beside him.

Harry opened the door to the tavern and walked in followed by Billy and Spike. Harry's blood pressure rose when he looked at all the men sitting at the bar. He spotted a dimly lit table far away from the bar. He directed Billy and the dog to it. They sat down and Harry looked over at Billy. "Well we're in the Topsy-Turvy so what's the big deal.?"

"Please don't talk just listen." Billy had his head cocked so his right ear was pointed at the bar. Harry looked at him then to the bar. Billy was listening to the guys sitting up there. He heard those guys threatening one another. Calling each other names referring to the private parts of the human body, and sex acts. All this was mixed with good old fashion cuss words.

A big smile came across Billy's. face. "Harry do you hear that? It's like a beautiful song to me."

"Are you nuts?"

"No. Harry, I'm not nuts. For the past eight years all I've had conversations with were doctors, nurses, teachers, and my family. Everyone has been super nice and polite. They call me Mister, or Billy in a kind tone. There is always someone there to help me. If I go to open a door someone does it for me. If I try to go downstairs someone grabs my elbow. I feel I'm a burden, and the only reason they're doing this for me is they feel sorry for me. Are they really sincere! It makes me feel uneasy. Now listen to those guys at the bar. They're telling each other how they really feel. Even though they're telling each other they hate and want to kill one another they're telling the truth and they mean it."

"Yeah, I hear them. It tells me there is going to be one hell of a fight in here. Let's get going."

Billy put up his hands. "No, please Harry, let's stay."

"Like I told you right from the start. This place is trouble. If we stay, were going to get caught up in a big mess. I can't fight a bunch of these guys."

"Hey, don't worry. I work out every day. I'm still strong. I know I can handle myself. Besides, we got Spike he's good for at least two of them."

"Billy, you not only lost your eyesight, you lost your brains. These guys will kill us. Come on, let's get out of here."

A loud yell from the bar got Harry's attention. A huge guy was standing up pointing his finger at another man. His other hand was rolled up into a fist. He was really mad. He shouted. "I'll break every bone in your rotten body if I ever hear you talk about my Rita again."

Harry got to his feet and was about to lift Billy up and pull him out of there. It was too late. Billy had taken off his dark glasses and had cupped his hands around his mouth. He yelled. "Hey big mouth, I had Rita out and she didn't show me much. I bought her a bar of soap. She hasn't washed in a year. If you come over here you won't see Rita again."

Harry's eyes came wide open. "Oh my God. Billy, that guy is big. I heard about him. He's tough and crazy. Pretend like you didn't say anything. If he looks over here I'll point at another guy at a different table."

Another loud yell from the bar. "Where you at you yellow bastard? I'll pull your tongue out of your head."

Harry stared at the guy then looked down to Billy. Billy shouted back. "Over here, big mouth. You better not come here because if you do that tramp Rita will be going to your funeral."

The big guy saw Harry standing up. He rushed from the bar knocking chairs, and tables over grunting and cursing. A group of his friends followed him. Harry looked down at Billy. He again had his head cocked. His face, had a strained look. His right ear was aimed at the big mad-man rushing toward them. Harry clenched his fists and planted his feet. There would be no talking to this guy. He had to give him his best punch.

The guy was about five feet away and still charging. Harry was about to hit him when a blur erupted from the table. Billy had come out of his chair like a spring that broke loose from its fasteners. Billy hit the guy flush in the face knocking him into tables and chairs. Billy dove on top of him immediately. His arms were swinging like propellers. One of the guys following the mad-man was about to jump on Billy. Harry hit him in the stomach, then in the face. The rest of the gang was ready to jump in. Billy heard them. He shouted. "Get em, Spike." The dog jumped completely over Billy and rushed the group. They saw the powerful-German Shepherd showing his teeth coming after them. They ran and climbed onto the bar.

Harry heard the sirens. "Come on, Billy we got to get out of here." Billy and the guy on the floor didn't pay any attention. They kept fighting. The police came in with their clubs in their hands, and whistles blowing. Billy and the mad-man slowly got to their feet. The big guy put a bottle of beer next to his swollen eye.

He looked at the officers. "I didn't do anything. I was just sitting at the bar not doing anything. All at once, this jerk starts a fight. The officers stared at Billy's face. Billy slowly started walking to his table. His hands were out in front of him feeling his way. He tripped on an overturned chair. He pulled himself up by grabbing the table. He rubbed his hands across the table til he found his dark glasses. He put them on and didn't say anything. Spike stood next to him.

The Officers looked at one another. They whispered "He's blind." They stared at the big guy and gave him a mean look.

The big guy shouted. "Hey I don't care what he is. I'd knock his ears out. Look what he did to my face. I'm missing a tooth. This is a bunch of shit. He's from the north end. Everyone of those guys are trouble." A big smile came across Billy's face.

Harry convinced the officers they were leaving and

they would not return. The officers took the madman outside. They explained it would be pretty hard to convince a Jury that he was beat up by a blind man.

Harry, Billy, and Spike got in the car and headed back to the north end. It was very quiet till Harry said. "Just look at you, Billy your face is all bruised, your lip is bleeding, and your hand is all swelled up. What did it prove?"

Billy didn't say anything for awhile. He just rubbed his swollen hand and had a slight smile." Harry, it proved a lot to me. I want to thank you."

Sea Monster In The Maumee River

It's 1:30 A.M. The water in the Maumee River is dark and calm. The moon is full, reflecting a silver streak across the surface. On the west bank sits three young boys around a fire. Their fishing lines are in the water. One looks at the others and says, "I bet I could swim across this river."

"Well, I got a dollar that says you can't."

Hearing this the first youth takes off his clothes and yells, "Your on." He wades into the water and is ready to start swimming.

One of the boys shouts. "Hey, how will we know you swam to the other side? You might go half way and turn around."

The boy in the water points to the other shore. "You see that fire over there? When I get there I'll pick up one of those burning logs and wave it back and forth." The other youths agree and the swimmer disappears into the darkness.

On the East bank sit four men huddled around a fire. Their voices carry far on this dark quiet, night. One of them could be heard. "These catfish sure aren't biting tonight." A long silence and suddenly a loud shout. "Man there must be a big one out there. I can hear him breaking water." More splashing and the men are all standing up with their hands

127

cupped over their eyes in an effort to see in the darkness.

The young swimmer is now about fifty yards off shore. He sees the four men silhouetted against the fire. He hears a voice from the group. "Shit man, I see it and it sure ain't no catfish. It's big and it's headed our way."

The young man is not only a good swimmer, he also has a sense of humor. He fills his mouth with water, and starts to give off loud gargling sounds. He almost chokes from laughing when he sees the four figures go crashing into the underbrush. His feet touch the bottom and he wades to the shore. He's still laughing as he goes to the fire and pulls out a burning log. He raises it above his head and swings it back and forth. The light reveals fishing equipment. The men in their hasty departure didn't take time to take their poles and tackle boxes.

The swimmer thought for awhile then he noticed a wooden door to a house that must have drifted up on the shore. He pushes the door into the water and puts the fishing poles and tackle boxes on top of it. Grabbing the rear section of the door, he starts to kick his legs like an outboard motor, and sets his course for the fire on the other shore where his friends are waiting.

The four fishermen ran to Tony Packo's restaurant at Front and Consaul St. and called the police.

Unit #2 pulls up and the fishermen run to them swearing and shouting.

"We were fishing and this big monster came after us. It was making loud roaring noises."

The officer asked. "What was it?"

Almost in unison they shouted. "Shit man, I wasn't sticking around to let that thing get close to me."

The officers listen to the whole story then drove to the Creig Bridge which was right above where the men were fishing. They leaned over the railing and played their powerful spotlight on the water. Below they saw some thing large with propulsion behind it. It didn't go under when the light struck it, but appeared to go faster. It seemed it was headed for the west bank. The officers ran up the walk to get a better look. They now made out it was a person kicking behind a board.

They ran back to their vehicle and drove to a dirt road that went to the bank of the west shore. The officers doused the headlights and quietly walked to the fire. The boys were helping the young swimmer pull the wooden door with the fishing poles and tackle boxes onto the shore. The officers stood by silently and listened.

"Man, I scared the hell out of some dudes fishing on the other side. They hauled ass when they heard me coming up on them. They left all this stuff." The boys were all laughing till one looked around and saw the reflection of the fire on the officers silver badges. He quickly grabbed his fishing pole and sat down. The other boys looked at him and he secretly pointed his finger behind him. They looked, saw the officers and froze in place. It became very quiet.

The officers stepped forward. "How's the fish biting tonight boys? You guys didn't happen to see any monsters?

We got a report there's something in the river that is getting ready to attack. Aren't you guys scared being down here with that thing near by?"

No one answered. The officer pointed to the boy who was wet. "You were swimming in the same water with that thing. You could have been eaten by it."

The boy just stared at the ground. "Sir, I'm sorry, I was just having a little fun. I didn't mean to scare those guys. I promise there won't be anymore trouble. All we want to do is fish the rest of the night."

The officers explained how dangerous the stunt was. They would give them a break this time and let them fish but they would be checking on them through out the night.

The boys thanked the officers and helped them carry the men's fishing equipment to the police vehicle. The officers returned to the fishermen and gave them back their equipment. They had a hard time explaining the sea monster without laughing.

Stimulant on Honeymoon Night

After many months of dreaming and planning, the big day finally arrived. All the preparations had paid off. The wedding was beautiful and the ceremony was conducted without a flaw.

The reception at the large hall had a merry atmosphere with the drinks and food plentiful. Marcia in her white gown and Jim dressed in a tux glided across the dance floor in rhythm with the soft music. He looked down into her dreamy eyes and said, "Let's leave the hall as soon as possible."

"Yes, honey," She giggled, "I know what you mean, They continued to dance and whisper to each other about what was going to happen later on.

At the bar stood Mike and Ben, keeping the bartender busy filling their glasses. They stared at the newlyweds on the dance floor. Mike smiled. "You know Ben, we ought to give them something to remember this night."

"What you getting at Mike?"

"Well, look at Jim out there. He looks like he's in another world. He needs a little excitement."

"Yeah, I see what you mean. What you want to do? Maybe we should mess with his car so he can't get to the motel."

"No, I've got a better idea. Let's go to the motel and wait for them."

"Well what we going to do when we get there?"

"Just have a few more drinks and I'll handle the motel scene."

The two young men watched every move the couple made. From the looks on the newly weds faces they knew they were going to sneak out as early as they could.

An hour passed and Mike hit Ben on the back. "Let's get out of here, we got to get to that motel before they do."

On the way to the motel Mike looked at Ben. "Do you know their room number?"

"No, I just heard they were staying at Happy Motel. How we going to find out what room they're in?"

The car did a sharp turn and stopped next to a phone booth. Mike jumped out of the car and grabbed the phone book. His fingers went to his mouth moistening them. He leafed through the pages. "Here it is, Happy Motel." A dime made a clinging noise then Mike dialed. Ben listened from the car.

"Yes sir, this is Jim Parker. I just got married today and in the excitement I forgot the number of our room." Silence then - "Number sixteen, I want to thank you sir. I'll be seeing you shortly." He got back in the car. "Ben, remember number sixteen. That's the room they're staying in. Let's go, we got work to do."

Mike parked the car in a dark area of the parking lot.

They entered through the back door of the motel. When they got in front of room sixteen Mike looked both ways then took his plastic driver's license out of his wallet. He inserted it into the door jam where the lock was located. After jiggling the card a few times the door opened.

Ben's eyes opened wide. "Hey that was cool the way you opened that door."

"Never mind, get inside and don't turn on the lights."

"Mike, now we're inside what we going to do?"

"We get under the bed and don't make any noise." He dropped to his knees and rolled over on his back and slid under the bed. "Come on Ben, get under here with me."

Ben got on his back and slid next to Mike. "Now that were under here, what in the hell are we going to do?"

"We wait under here till they get going good. You know what I mean. Then we push this mattress straight up."

"Man, Mike, I don't know about that. Marcia will become unglued. That girl has a terrible temper. I hope Jim don't have a gun."

The more they talked about it the more they laughed. The conversation and laughter stopped abruptly when they heard the click of the lock and the door swing open.

"Marcia, my beautiful bride, let me carry you across the threshold. I can't wait to see what this wonderful night has in store for us."

"Oh Jim, you are so romantic. Hurry let's get into our own little love pad."

The two under the bed are elbowing each other and

biting their lips trying not to laugh.

A cork from a champagne bottle pops. "Here's to the most beautiful wife in the world. Let's get out of these stiff clothes."

"That's the best thing I heard all night."

A short silence and the ruffling of clothes then the clinking of the glasses again. "To us Marcia, the best looking couple ever."

"Yes, honey you are so right. I do think were doing too much talking. We can do that later."

"I understand, beautiful."

All conversation between the newlyweds was now very intimate. The two under the bed continued to elbow each other when they heard this.

A whooshing sound and a large bump formed on the underside of the mattress. Ben looked at Mike and whispered. "Now?"

Mike shook his head no, and put his finger to his lips indicating he wanted him to be quiet.

A short time passed and the bed was creaking. Moaning and excited talk filled the room. Mike looked at Ben, smiled and pointed to the mattress above. He put his hands on it and waited for Ben to do the same.

A loud shout from under the bed. "PUSH IT BEN, PUSH HIGHER, HIGHER, GIVE IT ALL YOU GOT!" The mattress was now elevated and rocking like a raft in a storm.

Jim's voice from above. "What, what the hell is going

on?" Marcia screamed as she held on.

Mike shouted again, "GET IT HIGHER BEN!"

"I can't it's getting away from me. It's too heavy." His arms folded and his side of the mattress slammed down. Mike kept his side up, Jim and Marcia slid down, hit the floor and immediately bounced to their feet and grabbed anything that wasn't fastened and threw it at the two men on the floor. The pranksters grabbed the mattress and used it as a shield and backed out the door. They ran down the hall to the exit with the naked couple chasing with champagne bottles in their hands.

The scout car pulled into the driveway of the motel. It's bright headlights illuminated a naked woman standing defiantly in front of a car with two men inside. The windshield had been shattered. The officers quickly exited their car and ran to the woman. She screamed. "Let me tell you what these two sick, perverted sons of bitches did."

BOB MORRISSEY

Sickle Man

Three thirty in the morning and the calls finally slacked off. Howard the veteran officer was driving. He looked over at Carl, the rookie who was aiming the beam of his flashlight on the clip board. His finger was pointing at the entries on the log sheet. "Man, we answered twenty two calls so far, this is great."

Howard thought to himself. Rookies are all alike. They can't get enough. Wait till he gets twenty years on this job. He won't be asking for more. Carl turned the flashlight off, and immediately his eyes were scanning out the window looking for something suspicious.

Howard had twenty years on unit eleven, the hottest car in the city. Over the years he learned how to pace himself and not get burned out. He knew you don't move too fast on this car. If you do, chances are you won't be going home in the morning. This was the roughest part of town. The people here would shoot or knife you in a second. He looked over at his partner whose head was still turned toward the side window. "Hey Carl, let's get a sandwich, and a cup of coffee before the bullshit starts up again."

Carl didn't answer right away. Finally he said. "Well

all right."

Howard knew from the tone of Carl's voice that he didn't want to stop. He hadn't had his fill yet. "Listen kid, it will only take us a few minutes to grab a bite and we'll get back to the beat."

Again the answer was slow to come. "Yeah, it's all right with me."

Howard thought, I don't care if it's alright with you or not. I'm getting something to eat. He headed to the all night restaurant. No words were exchanged till Carl pointed and shouted. "Over there, that guy standing with his back against the wall looking over his shoulder."

The older officer stared at his partner then to the man leaning against the wall. "What the hell did he do? There's no law for leaning against a wall."

"He's suspicious, I bet he's a lookout the way he's staring over his shoulder."

"Everybody in this neighborhood looks over their shoulder. They want to know who's sneaking up on them. They want to be ready for the sucker who is going to rob them."

Carl wouldn't listen to any explanation. He was bound and determined he was going to check this guy out.

Howard shook his head. "When we go up on this guy we have to have a reason to check him out. Just looking suspicious is not a reason. If you want to see him move I'll show you how to do that."

Howard grabbed the spotlight from the dash board. He

played the beam in between the buildings, then crossed the center line and pulled up to the man leaning on the building. He brought the light on him. "Come here please, we'd like to talk with you."

"I ain't done shit honkey. Why you putting the hassle on me for? I'm just standing here and you put the big light on me. Ain't this a bitch."

Howard knew he was going to get this reaction. He felt like telling the rookie to get out and talk with the man and let him catch the flack. He had second thoughts because he knew what would happen. "Now listen man, all I want to do is ask you a question. It may save your life."

The man stared at Howard with a mean look. "What you mean, may save my life?"

"Well I wanted to ask you if you saw a man about six foot three, two hundred and fifty pounds, with a lot of hair piled up on his head. His eyes are so bloodshot they light up in the dark. He is naked, and carrying a sickle. He likes to wait behind trees and when someone comes down the sidewalk he chops their throat. The last guy he got he almost decapitated. Every time his heart beat, a stream of blood shot out of his juggler six feet high."

"No shit man? He go for the throat with a damn sickle. What they let a fool like that run?"

"Well he was a patient at the Mental Hospital. He's so strong he pulled the door right off the hinges and escaped. They say he sharpened that sickle like a razor."

The guy was now feeling his neck, and looking over

his shoulder. "Shit man, carry me over to the Flame restaurant?"

"Sorry we can't do that. The only people we haul in this car is people we arrest."

"Man, that sorry son of a bitch might rip me with that damn sickle. You got to carry my ass out of here."

"Listen you can be a concerned citizen. We'd like to catch this guy before he cuts someone else's throat. Will you act as bait? You walk down the sidewalk and we'll follow. When he jumps out and tries to cut your head off we'll arrest him."

The man squinted with a frightened look. "Man, you're crazier then that fool with the sickle. Asking shit like that."

"Well we got to get going. If you see this guy give us a call."

"Man I don't want to see that sucker. If I do it won't be for long."

Both officers watched as the man broke and ran at full speed right down the middle of the street. Howard looked over at his young partner. "Is that fast enough for you?"

The Ugly One

Bob and Harold were the best of friends. Like most young men they enjoyed the wild side of life. Have a few drinks, then meet some good looking girls. Bob was the bigger of the two, about 6 foot, muscular build, and sort of good looking. Harold was thinner with average looks; he wore black horn-rimmed glasses. Both were shy with the girls until they had a few beers. Their motto was, "Drink a six pack and they all look alike."

Bob had a sure fire system for picking up the best-looking women. He and Harold would go to a bar. Bob drank his beer slowly while he encouraged his friend to chug his. Harold would get buzzed quick. Bob knew that and when Harold took off his black horn-rimmed glasses and placed them on the table it meant he was ready to meet some nice girl to dance with. Harold always made the first move on the ladies. He would ask a girl at a table to dance and if she accepted, Bob would go to the same table and ask her friend.

This night they were sitting at a table at the Paladrome Nite Club. Harold had fortified his courage with six bottles of beer. Bob watched him remove his glasses. Harold shouted "I'm ready, bring on the broads." He squinted, and tried to see a girl to dance with. Bob knew he could hardly see the people sitting at the next table, let alone the tables at the other end of the room. It was now time to work his plan like he had so many times before. He looked over all the tables and finally found the one he wanted. Two girls were sipping their drinks. one in a black sweater was a pretty blond. The other, dressed in a red blouse, was a very large girl, and not very good looking. Bob stared at his friend.

"Harold don't turn around right now. There's a couple of girls about five tables away. They're both looking at us. The one in the red blouse is pointing at you. I can read her lips. She said she thinks you're cute."

"No shit, Bob? Man, when I stand up just aim me toward that table. I'll dance with her and talk do-do and put a smile on her face that will look like she got a coat hanger stuck in her mouth."

Bob sort of felt guilty. The girls weren't looking at him and Harold, but what was the difference. Harold would go to that table and ask the homely one to dance. Odds were she would jump up and dance. It worked so many times before. The good looking one would be mad that Harold didn't ask her to dance first. She'd hate to sit there alone. He then would go to the table and ask her to dance. They never refused.

Bob watched the girl nod, then got up and grabbed Harold's hand. They both walked to the dance floor. Bob could not believe how tall this girl was. She must have been six foot three. He laughed when Harold squinted and looked up at her as they danced. The pretty blond at the table had an angry look. Bob patted his hair down with his hands and made his way to the table. He looked down at the girl. She was much prettier close up. "Would you care to dance?"

She smiled and said. "Yes, I would like that."

Bob slid the chair back so she could stand. *It never failed.* He had no problem finding Harold on the dance floor. The girl he was dancing with was the tallest person in the night club. Bob laughed when he saw Harold's head leaning on the girls chest, and she was looking down at the top of his head. Harold didn't care, he was in another world. After a few dances, the two couples left the dance floor. Bob and Harold accepted the girls invitation to join them at their table. The two guys felt pretty proud they had met the girls. They increased their drinking. Both of them were getting drunk, but the right words were coming out of their mouths. The girls smiled when the boys flattered them on how good looking they were.

As the evening passed, the dancing and drinking continued. Everyone was having a good time and plans were made to go out after the bar closed. Carol, the girl Bob was sitting next to, asked. "Bob, do you come to this bar very often?"

He looked at her and the drinks answered for him. "Yes, Harold and me come here a lot. We pick up a lot of girls. I let Harold get drunk and then I sic him on some ugly broad. I then get the ugly girl's friend. It always works."

Harold hearing this, slowly put his glasses on and looked at the big girl who was staring at him.

"Damn. You are ugly."

The large girl sprang to her feet. Her fist hit Bob flush in the face and knocked him out of his chair. She pulled the glasses off Harold's face and punched him in the eye. "Who the hell do you creeps think you are?"

The bartender saw the big woman in action. He grabbed the phone. "Police, hurry get to the Paladrome Nite Club. An Amazon woman is tearing up the place."

A Rookie's First Incident

Standing in formation at roll call, the young man waited for his first assignment. He looked around and noticed most of the officers were seasoned. A few were rookies and some of them had graduated from the academy with him. He laughed when he looked at the older officers' pants. At the academy the instructors often said, "You're not a veteran till the back of your pants shine." His name was called and he shouted. "Here Sir."

"You got Summit and Cherry and you hit the call box on the hour."

He thought, oh good, Skid Row, lots of action. It then dawned on him that he would be by himself. No instructor standing next to him, making sure he made the right decision. He felt his pockets to make sure he had his notes in case he needed them.

Meanwhile in an alley called Ostrich Lane, a local drunk stared at his second bottle of cheap wine. He had polished off the first one five minutes ago. He debated with himself if he should drink it right away. It was a short debate. He flung his head back and put the bottle to his lips. Large bubbles erupted inside as the wine drained down his throat. He felt the effects immediately. Fear flashed in his

145

mind. He thought of the last time he was arrested. The judge pointed at him and said. "Next time you come into this court for being drunk I'm going to give you six months."

Six months wouldn't be bad in the winter. But it's spring now and who wants to be in jail when it's warm. He threw the empty bottle down and staggered out of the alley onto Cherry Street.

The young officer felt conspicuous with his new uniform on. As he walked past the large businesses he looked at his reflection to reassure himself he was really a policeman. His head quickly turned from the windows to a lady running up to him screaming.

"Officer, Officer" She grabbed his shirt. Hurry a man is hurt bad."

"Where is he."

She pointed and ran. He followed her to where a man was lying on the sidewalk. The drunk saw the uniform coming to him. He thought, if he didn't get up he'd have to face that judge who was going to give him six months in jail. He tried to get to his feet but the wine had control over him. It was no use, he'd have to stay on the sidewalk. He squinted his bloodshot eyes and saw the officer was a rookie. He quickly grabbed his side and made a painful look on his face.

The young officer dropped to his knee. "What's the matter mister?"

"I've been shot."

HUMOROUS BEAT

The rookie jumped up and ran to the call box. He shouted into the phone. "Operator, send me an ambulance. I got a man shot." The district crew and the ambulance pulled up to the scene with their sirens blaring and lights flashing. The man was put on a stretcher and quickly put in the ambulance. It drove off at a high rate of speed for the hospital. The district crew along with the rookie followed.

At the hospital a doctor walked up to the officers. "Which one of you sent the man here?"

The rookie pointed to himself. "I did sir."

"Well, that man is not shot."

"Not shot? I saw him on the ground holding his side. He looked in bad shape. He said he was shot."

"Well, I examined him and I can't find any wound." The doctor pointed to the room the drunk was in. "Go see for yourself. If you see a bullet hole, let me know."

The rookie dashed into the room. He shouted. "Where you shot?"

The drunk pointed at an old scar on his side and slurred. "Right here."

"That's an old wound. What the hell is the matter with you? Why did you lie to me?"

The drunk raised both his hands. "I didn't lie to you. I said, I'd been shot. It happened four years ago. You never asked me when it happened."

The rookie kept staring at him with a disgusted look. The older officers walked up to him and patted him on the back. "Don't let it bother you. It happened to all of us when we were new."

The rookie felt the back of his pants and mumbled. "I can't wait till you shine."

You Won't Believe This

Arnold got off work and thought how hot it had been working on that furnace, molding glass. He wanted to stop at his usual tavern but not today. He had his new car and didn't want anything to happen to it. All his life he waited for this car. One that had the new smell and all the accessories. He wouldn't have to lean forward anymore when someone got in the back seat. This car had four doors.

He carefully parked the car in front of his home. He admired it when he got out then walked to the neighborhood bar. He didn't particularly like this bar because it wasn't the cleanest place in town. It was called the Frontier. The woman who ran it was called Dirty Legs. She was about eighty years old and skinny. The only clothing anyone ever saw her wear was a thin, soiled slip. It hung on her as if it was on a hanger. She had to slide when she walked. The house slippers she wore were almost as old as she was. They were broken down and worn. If she tried to walk, her feet would come out of them. Her hair was gray and unkept. A lit cigarette constantly dangled from her mouth and the front of her tangled hair was yellow from the nicotine that drifted up. On many occasions drunks would heave on the bar. Dirty Legs would use her forearm like a squeegee and slide it away and get him another drink.

Arnold pulled out a barstool and sat down. Dirty Legs shuffled to him. Her head was cocked and one eye was shut trying to duck the curling smoke coming from the cigarette stuck between her lips. "What you have, stud?"

"I'd like a shot and a beer in clean glasses."

She looked at him funny. "I got something better then whiskey. It's called Kentucky White."

"What's Kentucky White? I never heard of it."

"You know, white lightening. It's cheap and good. Some guy from the hills makes it."

"I'll give it a try." Dirty Legs brought the drinks and waited till he paid. Arnold raised the Kentucky White and drained it. He was surprised. It had a good taste and went down smooth. Dirty legs watched the satisfied look on his face and shouted, "Want another one, stud?" Arnold raised the empty glass and nodded his head. This scene was repeated a few more times.

A friend of Arnold's came in and sat next to him. The skinny little woman dragged her feet and stood in front of him. She gave him the pitch to buy moonshine. "No. I don't want that crap. It'll make you go blind." He looked at Arnold. "Man, you ain't drinking that shit are you?"

Yea, I like it. First time I ever had it."

"Well, maybe it'll be the last time you do. That stuff will kill you. Some hill goon probably made it in a still just as dirty as this joint."

Arnold didn't heed the warning. He kept putting it

away till his vision turned blurry. He knew it was time to get out of there. He staggered home. A few times he had to grab trees to steady himself. He stood in front of his home and looked at his new car. He thought, I just want to hear that powerful motor purr one more time. He stumbled to his car and managed to get inside. That was the last thing he remembered.

The silence in the neighborhood was pierced by loud screams. Someone called the police. The scout car pulled up in front of Arnold's house. Neighbors who had congregated on the sidewalk pointed to Arnold's car. One officer walked to the driver's side of the car. The other went to the rear of it. The one behind yelled to his partner. "Bob, come here. You won't believe this." Bob ran to the back of the car. His partner pointed to a man sobbing in the rear seat. He had a key in his hand and was trying to poke it into the back of the front seat. One of the officers shouted at the man inside, "What's the matter with you? Why are you yelling?"

A slurred voice cried out. "Some dirty thief stole my steering wheel on my new car."

The officer named Bob shook his head. "This guy is so drunk he don't know he's in the back seat."

BOB MORRISSEY

Live Sardines

An old car came to a stop near the Maumee River and the small cloud of dust that had been following engulfed it. Ben quickly got out and waved the dust away from his face. "Hurry up, Leroy, them fish are just waiting to be caught." Both men unloaded the fishing equipment from the trunk and hurried to their usual spot on the bank.

Leroy shouted, "Get them minnows into the water before they die." Ben grabbed the chain and tied it to a dead tree. He then threw the metal bucket containing the minnows into the river. Both men sat down, baited their hooks and cast their lines in the water.

An hour passed with no bites. "Hey Ben, what you got in them bags you brought?"

"I got some sardines and two gallons of homemade grape wine."

"Homemade grape wine. Let's have a nip of that stuff. That's going to make my day."

Ben reached into the bag and pulled out the large containers. He unscrewed one of the caps and raised the gallon jug to his mouth with both hands. The purple liquid slid down his throat. Large bubbles shot up inside the jug. He brought the bottle down, wiped his mouth with his shirt

153

sleeve and shouted. "Wow, that stuff got a punch." He passed the jug to Leroy's waiting hands. Leroy followed suit. After he got his fill he passed it back to Ben. This continued till the jug was empty. They then opened the other jug.

"Ben, I got a great idea. Instead of going fishing, let's go drinking."

"That's the smartest thing you ever said, Leroy old buddy. Go back in them bags and bring out those cans of sardines."

Leroy struggled to his feet and staggered to the bags. His head wobbled a couple of times above them before his hand dove in and pulled out five cans of sardines. One can fell and he tried to catch it. He lost his balance and slipped backwards. He didn't try to get up. Instead he crawled back to his pole, pushing the cans in front of him. In a slur, he said. "You know, Ben, those sardines will go great with this wine."

Ben smiled. "Anything goes good with wine." He grabbed one of the cans, opened it and started eating the sardines.

About fifty yards away, two modern day Tom Sawyers were rafting the river. The younger one saw the men fishing. "Come on, let's go see if they caught anything."

The boys startled the men when they poled up behind them and shouted. "Hey mister, did you catch anything?"

Ben's head jerked slightly and looked at the boys. "Yea, we caught two dozen. They're at the end of that chain."

The boys quickly grabbed the chain and pulled in the bucket. One of them shouted. "Hey, these ain't fish, they're minnows."

Hearing this Ben and Leroy laughed so hard they had to hold their stomachs. Ben slurred, "You see, boys, we went into the bait store and the man gave us a net. He said, give me a dollar and you can catch two dozen. I took the net and I caught every one of them." The men again laughed when they saw the expressions on the boys faces.

Leroy grabbed an open can of sardines and showed it to the boys. "You see these? We caught them yesterday." Again the men broke out laughing.

The boys stared at them. The older one turned to his friend. "These guys are drunk. Lets have some fun." They watched the men eat the sardines and drink the wine.

One of the boys reached into the minnow bucket and pulled out a handful of the small lively fish. The other shouted, "I think you got a bite." Both men grabbed their poles and stared for movement on their lines. The boy put the minnows into the open sardine cans.

Ben put his pole back down. "That wasn't a damn bite."

The boys waited patiently for the men to eat more sardines. Finally Leroy reached into the can and pulled out one of the minnows. He almost got it to his mouth but it squirmed away and dropped to the ground. He stared at it, them dropped to his knees and cupped it. With both hands he managed to get it in his mouth. The boys laughed when they saw the movement of his cheeks and jaw. His teeth couldn't catch the moving minnow. He grabbed the grape wine and flushed it down. Again he reached into the can and pulled out a handful of minnows mixed with sardines. He quickly put them in his mouth and swallowed. He did this a couple more times and Ben shouted. "Hey man, save some for me. I'm the one who bought them."

Leroy stared at him with a mean look. "Man, you don't need to yell. Here take your damn sardines." He slid the can next to Ben.

Ben reached and took one of the minnows from the can. In his stupor he wasn't aware the small fish was alive. The minnow jumped from his hand and landed in his shirt pocket. He squinted, looking for it. He shrugged his shoulders and reached back into the can and took out another one. He managed to push the fluttering fish into his mouth with the palm of his hand. Leroy stared at Ben's lips where the tail of the minnow was sticking out flapping. He laughed. "Hey man that's cool. How do you make that tail do that? It looks like it's alive."

Ben spit the minnow into the river and it immediately swam away. His eyes came wide open. The minnow in his shirt pocket flipped out and landed in the water. It too swam away.

Ben stared at Leroy, who was laughing. He grabbed him by the shirt collar. "So you want to be a wise guy. Well wise guy, how do you like this?" Both men were now tangled up, punching each other. Seeing this, the two boys ran.

"Unit #1. At the Middle Ground Park by the river a disturbance. Two men fighting."

BOB MORRISSEY

What's It All About?

Day after day at the Police Academy I dreamed about my first day on the street, when the umbilical cord would be cut and I would be on my own. After all those weeks of training I'd be turning on the red lights and siren and getting involved in high speed chases. Catching a robber, or a burglar and maybe even a murderer. At every lecture concerning crime my imagination would draw pictures of me solving them. I could not wait.

Graduation day finally came. We cadets took our first step to becoming officers. We stood tall in our new uniforms. We caterpillars had turned into butterflies. The next day we would be alone on the street.

My first assignment was walking a beat in Skid Row. The area was made up of cheap bars, rundown hotels and flop houses. The people were down and out and most of them were alcoholics. The crime rate was high.

I felt a little awkward as I walked down the street in my uniform. I had the feeling everyone was staring at my new uniform and thinking, now there's a real rookie. I kept looking at my reflection in the large windows making sure my uniform was proper. I thought I had to do something to get rid of this rookie image. I remembered seeing veteran officers swinging their billy clubs back and forth then catching it after it did a couple of flips in front of them.

I unhooked my club and wrapped the leather strap around my hand. I flung it in front of me and it came right back to my palm making a nice slapping sound. I did it a couple more times and I felt proud. I started walking with a little swagger and increased the speed of the club flipping out of my hand. I was gaining confidence until I was distracted and my eyes left the club. It came back hard striking me across the knuckles. Sharp pain drew tears to my eyes. I tried to be casual. I hoped no one had seen me do this. My hand hurt so bad but I wouldn't grab it for fear someone had seen me get whacked. I quickly ducked into the hallway of an apartment building. I threw my head back, clenched my teeth, grabbed my throbbing hand and massaged it.

I stood in this position rocking back and forth mumbling words I don't normally use when I heard, "Good morning officer."

Standing in front of me was a little old lady staring. I tried to force a smile and I said. "Good morning ma'am. Unconsciously I grabbed the door with my injured hand to let her out. When it made contact with the door knob it felt like a lighting bolt shooting up my arm. I let out a yelp. She jumped back. I grabbed the knob with my good hand and opened the door. She quickly exited, all the time looking at me with a strange expression.

Back on the sidewalk I kept my eyes peeled for anything which looked suspicious. I kept thinking, when will it happen? Will it be a robbery, fight, or maybe a murder. Hours passed I was getting tired of standing and waiting for something to happen. I leaned against a building and watched the traffic go by. I was ready to give up expecting anything exciting to happen when I heard loud shouting. "Officer, officer, help." I quickly turned my head to the sound of that voice. A man was running toward me. His arms were flailing and he was screaming in broken English.

I ran to him shouting. "What is the matter?" He didn't answer. He turned and ran to a beat up apartment building. I chased after him. He yanked open the front door and motioned for me to go in. He climbed the stairs two at a time. The building smelled musty, the wallpaper was the color of nicotine. A light bulb dangled from a frayed cord at the top of the steps.

When I got to the second floor the excited man was standing next to an open door. He pointed inside. I cautiously entered. It was a one room apartment. Nothing was moving except a small fan straining to move the stale air. The nervous man pointed to a bed with a very old gentleman lying on it. "He very sick. He very sick," he kept repeating. "He want you." Quickly I went to the bed. The old man was very still. His eyes were frosted and unfocused. I put my ear close to his mouth to see if he was breathing. His hand slowly rose up and pressed against my chest. He groped back and forth till he found my badge. He squeezed it and held on. A faint smile came on his face. His hand slid down my arm to my hand and he held tight.

161

I was lost for words but somehow I knew what was happening. I didn't move. I continued to hold his hand till the grip faded and his hand went limp. There was nothing I could do for him. Then I looked at the peaceful smile on his face and I realized I had already done what he wanted. He knew that his time on this earth had come down to a few minutes. He wanted someone at his side he could trust. Someone who cared and would look after him and his meager belongings. I said a prayer and slowly put his hand back at his side. I nodded at him and said in a low voice, "Thanks, old man, you taught me what this uniform is about."

Resurrection Day

Hank pulled out his wallet and quickly slid out his drivers license. He looked at his birth date on the license and then to the calendar. He shouted out. "Hot dam, I'm now a man. No more drinking that three two beer that tastes like Kool Aid. A man drinks fire water and a beer chaser. Whiskey, that is what this adult male is going to drink from now on. I'll show them guys at the bar this man can handle the high power stuff. When you're twenty one you are suppose to act like a man. And that means drinking like a man."

In front of the Riverside Tavern he again pulled out his drivers license studied it for a little while, slapped it in the palm of his hand, and put it in his shirt pocket so he would have it ready when Eddie the bartender tried to give him a beer. He pulled the door with authority. He stuck out his chest and strutted in. A few of his friends yelled to him to come sit with them at a table. He gave them a funny look and yelled "No way, this man is sitting up at the bar close to the source."

Eddie saw Hank coming and drew him a glass of beer. Hank pulled the stool away from the bar with his foot and

163

sat down. He pulled out his drivers license and held it for Eddie to examine. He slid the glass of beer away from him. "No more am I drinking that panther piss. I'm a man and I want whiskey." Eddie stared at him and smiled then handed him back his license.

"Well big man what is it going to be?" Hank looked at the other guys sitting next to him. He made sure he had all their attention before he answered.

"I want a whiskey and a mug of beer." He then looked at the guys again. They were quiet and had smiles on their faces. Eddie placed a shot of whiskey, and a mug of beer in front of him. Hank picked up the whiskey in the small glass. He held it up then toasted the guys to the right, then to the left. He shouted, "Over the lips, over the gums. Look out belly here it comes." He slung his head back, put the small glass to his lips and drained it. He slammed the glass down on the bar, and wiped his mouth with his shirt sleeve just like in the movies. "Another one bartender."

Hank tried to act cool but the burning sensation in his mouth and throat was unbearable. He tried to act like it was not affecting him. His eyes were watering, and his mouth was wide open. A loud Ahhhh noise came out of him when he exhaled. He quickly grabbed the large mug of beer and gulped it as fast as he could in hopes of extinguishing the fire within him.

Everyone at the bar was laughing. He saw this and he quickly gained his composure. He didn't care how much it burned. His feelings were hurt and he was going to prove he was a man. Eddie was still standing in front of him laughing. "Did I hear you say you wanted another one?"

"Your damn right I want another one. This time make it a double shot."

Eddie twisted his mouth and winked his eye. "You sure you want another one?"

"Your dam right I want another one. Here's my money and here's my I.D. Now bring me that double."

Eddie brought Hank his whiskey, only this time a double and in a much larger glass. He looked Hank in the eye. "Listen kid you never drank whiskey before. Why don't you take it easy?"

"Hey Eddie I ordered whiskey not a lecture. Now no more of this kid talk. I'm a man and I want to drink like a man. Understood?"

Eddie shrugged his shoulders, made a disgusted look and said. "The customer is always right."

Hank thought he had the secret of drinking whiskey. Drink the whiskey straight down, before it has a chance to burn. You grab the mug of cold beer right away and wash it down. Eddie placed the double shot in front of him. He grabbed it and down it went. He quickly grasped the mug of beer and drained it. Every one was watching Hank for his reaction. He smiled and shouted. "Another one bartender. This man is thirsty."

The fast drinking continued. Eddie and Hank's friends tried to warn him to slow down. Hank would have none of this talk. "Listen you guys don't worry. I'm twenty one years old. A full grown adult male. This stuff won't affect me. I told you before I am legal, and I got money so keep it coming."

Fifteen minutes later Hank felt a strange sensation taking over his body. His sight started to blur. He had trouble understanding what people were saying to him. He stood up and was dizzy. He thought, get control, and get the hell out of here. He squinted and started to walk to the door, tried to go straight but it was no use. The upper part of his body was going faster then his lower part. The lower part was trying to catch up with the upper part and he bulldozed into the chairs and tables. He pulled himself up and people shouted, "You ok Hank?"

He motioned with his hand and said. "Yeah, every-thing is cool. I think I tripped over a loose tile." He thought got to get out side in the fresh air.

Outside he took some deep breaths. Everything looked strange. His legs started to move again but he couldn't direct them. He wandered aimlessly till he bumped into a large stone object. He tried to get around it but kept bump-ing into another one. He was in a maze. He felt like a pinball bouncing off them. He became tired and dropped to his knees and leaned back on the large stone and passed out.

Five hours later the sun began to rise and the birds started singing. Hank rolled over. He felt something strange. It was not his bed. It was grass. His bloodshot eyes slitted open. His head ached terribly. He squinted to the left, then to the right. His eyes exploded open. He was surrounded by tombstones. He covered his eyes and gave off with a loud scream.

"Unit #4 go to Forest Cemetery a man yelling for help." The two officers walked up to Hank who was sitting on a tombstone crying and shouting he was dead. They convinced him he was still alive even though he didn't feel like it.

After calming him down one of the officers looked at the other one. "Old Hank here thought it was resurrection day and he was the first one up."

BOB MORRISSEY

Worked Out

Tony placed a new gym bag on the kitchen table. His wife watched as he unzipped it and took out a pair of workout shorts, shirt, socks and shoes.

She stared at him. "What's this all about?"

Tony smiled at her. "I'm turning over a new leaf. I joined the "Y" and I'm going to get in shape. You won't know me when I get done."

"You never worked out before, why now?"

"Well you got to start sometime. I'm really in the mood, Betty, don't discourage me."

Betty went along with it. Weeks passed and she kept looking for some improvement in her husband's physical condition. Instead of losing weight he was gaining and looking puffy. Tony would leave the house at six o'clock every Monday, Wednesday, and Friday. The first couple of weeks he came home at ten o'clock. Then he began to come home later and later.

Tony thought he had a good thing going. It was the perfect alibi. Instead of going to the "Y", he was meeting his girl friend at a tavern. During the night he'd pick up his

169

gym bag and go to the rest room. Once inside he'd remove his workout shorts, shirt, and socks and place them under the faucet to soak them. He'd ring them out and wrap a towel around them and place the wet bundle back into the bag.

His girlfriend stared at him when he returned to the table. She'd ask, "Are you afraid I'm going to steal that bag when you go to the men's room? What do you have in there that's valuable?"

Tony just smiled and shook his head. "It's nothing like that. It's a little secret right now. Someday I'll tell you all about it. I'm sure you'll get a real laugh out of it."

After every workout Betty took his wet clothes from the bag and washed them. She thought he must really be exercising hard to perspire so much. She could not understand why he was not losing weight and became suspicious. The wet clothes didn't smell like someone had been exercising in them.

The next time Tony came home from his workout, Betty was waiting. He threw his gym bag on the floor and dropped into his overstuffed chair. "Boy I'm beat, I took it to the max. I never worked out so hard."

Betty didn't say anything. She walked to the gym bag and picked it up. She pulled out the gym shorts. He stared at her suspiciously. She held up the shorts and punched her fist into one of the leg holes. Her fist didn't come out. She threw the shorts in his face. "The only workout you could have had with these shorts would be a one legged man's ass kicking contest."

Tony grabbed the shorts and examined them. His eyes opened wide when he saw that someone had sewed the leg hole together. He felt this was not the time for talking. He jumped up and ran out the door.

"Unit #10, 1211 Dorr St. A demented woman beating a man with a gym bag."

BOB MORRISSEY

Different Worlds

November 11, 1968. Big Jim pulled up to the construction site. Through the swooping arms of the windshield wipers he saw the foreman in his yellow raincoat with a clipboard in his hand. As the foreman approached, Jim rolled down the window.

"Sorry, Jim, looks like this rain is going to last all day. I'll see you tomorrow."

Jim drove away, his mood as bad as the weather. He decided to stop at the local pub on the way home. He drew a stool away from the bar and sat down. A mug of beer slid in front of him. After a short conversation with the bartender, he was alone. He stared out the windowt, *everything sure is dismal at this time of the morning when it rains.* The drinks kept coming and the time drifted by. The bartender looked at the clock and automatically got a chair to stand on and turned on the T.V.

He looked at Jim. "Time for the news." Jim didn't respond. He kept staring at his glass, rubbing the moisture from it. Jim didn't pay attention to the news until he heard the Marine Corps Hymn. His eyes looked up at the T.V. The announcer said, "Let us not forget our veterans to whom we owe so much. Today is Veterans Day. Here are some of the scenes of past wars and parades." The spirited music caused Jim's fingers to go up and down on the bar keeping rhythm with it.

He remembered many years back, right after the sneak attack on Pearl Harbor, when he joined the Marines. How tough boot camp was. The ride overseas on the big ship to combat. His spirits picked up when he thought how lucky he was to be here. A lot of his buddies were not so fortunate. What a beautiful sight it was when the war was over and he came home to the United States. He can still visualize soldiers walking down the gang plank, with the band playing "God Bless America." Many of them dropped to their knees, tears streaming down their cheeks as they kissed the ground.

This was a day dedicated to him and all the other veterans. Jim felt proud. He arched his back and stuck out his chest. He was glad he had done his part. He would go again if called. He felt so much pride his body tingled. The music, beer, and memories continued. He sat at the bar with a contented smile. The reminiscing stopped abruptly when the silence was broken by a loud shout. "Peace, baby." Jim spun around and saw two young men sitting in a booth. Their hair was long and they had beards. Their arms were pointed upward with their fingers split to form a V. They were shouting to another young man who had entered. He too had a beard and a pony tail.

When he saw his friends he raised his arm and gave them a V sign and shouted, "Peace, baby."

Big Jim stared at them in disbelief. He mumbled under his breath. "Well, I'll be a son of a bitch." He got off the stool and walked over to the booth and stared at them. "What is this peace baby shit? Listen, you yellow hippie slope heads. I'm going to tell you what it's all about." His voice was loud and firm. In an almost perfect imitation of Winston Churchill, he shouted. "Never in the history of mankind have so many owed so much to so few. Now that, you yellow creeps, is what Winston Churchill said. Furthermore, he is the one who put up his two fingers to form a V. He meant that to be victory. Not peace baby. Now, jerks, if you want to put up a peace sign, be original and make a P with your fingers. What the hell school did you go to? Peace starts with a P not a V." Jim then raised his middle finger. "Here's my sign to you."

The three long-hairs jumped to their feet. one shouted, "You warmonger."

Big Jim stuck his finger in the man's chest. "Listen, creep, if it wasn't for us veterans you'd be speaking Japanese, and you'd have to get off your pot-smoking ass and work."

The argument now turned physical. Big Jim punched one of them and sent him spinning through the tables knocking them over like bowling pins. The other two jumped on Jim's back. Men at the bar rushed to join in the ruckus.

The bartender saw this and grabbed the phone and called the police. "Get me some help. My bar is being tore up."

The officers arrived and rushed to the bar. They could hear cursing and bottles breaking inside. They yanked opened the door. Men were entangled, rolling around on the floor punching one another. The officers pulled them apart. "There will be no more fighting! Who started this?"

The battlers rubbed their wounds and pointed at each other shouting about wars and other problems of the world.

One of the officers put up his hands. "Hold It, hold it. Were not the United Nations. Were just peace officers and were going to have peace, is that understood?" It became quiet. The combatants all nodded.

"Now, it looks like everything is under control. If it starts up again when we leave we'll come back. We got a man downtown in a black robe who's got the answers. He won't be in until tomorrow. You can cool off in the Iron Bar Motel. Is that understood?" The fighters nodded. The officers pointed their night sticks at them and left.

I'm Growing

It was a ritual, every morning the older detective came in forty five minutes early. Standing on his tip toes he would grasp the frayed string turning on the light over his desk. The old string was much shorter then it use to be. He had to pinch the end of it with his thumb and forefinger just to get hold of it.

After the light was lit Ed would go to the closet and get his worn out broom and carry it to his desk at port arms. He swept the whole area, then returned the broom to the closet, again at port arms. He always hung the broom on the same hook. Back at the desk he'd stare at the calendar, checking the date. He would then grab the desk and push it back and forth three times making sure it was in the right place. Arching his back he'd take a deep breath then let the air out with a whistling sound. He was now ready for work.

Two detectives from the midnight shift waiting to go home were watching him as they had done for months. Bill looked at his partner. "You know Phil, old Ed comes in every morning and does the same thing. It's like he's programmed. I looked at that broom of his and all the paint

177

is worn off where he grabs it. I wonder how many years he's been doing that?"

"Many years, probably before we were born. Take a look at that string, I wonder how long it used to be. He has to stand on his tiptoes so his fingers can get hold of it." They kept watching old Ed. Bill shook his head.

"I hope when I get that many years on this job I don't get crazy like that."

Days went by and Bill watched the old detective go through his routine every morning. He laughed to himself and thought it was time to test the old guy. That night when he came to work he brought a string, and a saw. At about four o'clock in the morning when the action stopped he took the broom from the closet. He pulled the broom stick out where it was attached to the straw. He sawed off a couple of inches then inserted it back into the broom.

Bill then climbed onto Ed's desk and removed the string from the light. He tied two more inches to the old string making sure it was the part that was closest to the light. He wanted Ed to see the stained, and frayed part of the string when he reached up to turn on the light.

He now turned the desk over on its side and sawed one inch off each leg. After cleaning the area he put the desk back on its legs. He looked at all the alterations that he made and was satisfied that there was no trace anything had been tampered with.

The next morning Old Ed came in forty five minutes early just like he had for thirty five years. He stood under the light and got on his tip toes and grabbed the string with his thumb and fore finger. He didn't pull it he just stared at the excess string extending down from his finger and thumb. Finally he pulled and lit the light. He backed away and stared at the string from different angles. Again he went back to the string. This time he stood flat-footed and grabbed it. He could not believe it. There was still string left over. He pulled many times turning the light on and off.

His partner of many years, Ben Murphy, was sitting at his desk trying to type a report. He shouted. "Leave that damn light on or off." Ed shrugged his shoulders and walked to the closet all the time looking back at the string. He got his broom and looked like a soldier carrying his rifle at port arms. Before he started sweeping he looked up at the string again with a puzzled expression.

He started to sweep and the upper part of his body bent forward and down. He pushed the broom away and stared at it. The broom was his. He continued to sweep, even though it felt strange, and the broom seemed shorter. He stopped, leaned on it, stared to the left, then to the right making sure no one was looking at him. He kept glancing from the broom to the string. He shook his head, mumbled, shrugged his shoulders, and returned the broom to the closet.

Pulling the chair away from his desk he sat down. He grabbed the desk as usual and pushed it forward then pulled it back. His eyes opened wide as the underside of the middle drawer rubbed across the tops of his knees. Immediately he pushed it forward and again it rubbed his knees.

Ed jumped up and ran to the window. He looked at his reflection. He stood straight and inspected himself from the front then turned around and looked over his shoulder checking his back side all the time talking to himself.

His partner, Ben squinted his eyes and stared at him. He slowly took the stub of cigar from his mouth and yelled. "What in the hell is the matter with you?"

Ed stared at him with a concerned look. "Ben, do I look taller? Do my clothes look like they fit me? Can a guy grow after he's sixty years old?"

"Ed, you don't grow taller after you're sixty. You grow crazy, you senile fool. You better quit this shit, or put in your papers for retirement. This job has finally gotten to you."

Hardening

I watched him check out the equipment to the scout car before we started our tour. Typical rookie, I thought. Going over every detail. Doing it by the book. Just like they taught him in the academy. I walked up to him and he threw out his hand. "I'm Pat Mc Carthy. They assigned me to you. I hope you don't mind working with a rookie?"

"No I don't mind as long as you don't get me killed driving this car." His eyes opened wide.

"You mean you're going to let me drive?"

"Yeah, you know how, don't you?"

"Oh yes, I know how, but most older officers don't let new guys drive right away."

"Just be careful when you turn on those red lights and siren. Most people will pull over, but some don't see or hear them. I don't want to get killed. I want to go home when we get off. Not the hospital or morgue."

"Yeah, I know all about that. They warned us about hot calls in the academy. Don't worry, I'll be careful."

I sat back and Pat drove. The radio broke the silence. I saw his knuckles get white gripping the steering wheel. "Is that us?"

"No, that's not us. I'll let you know. Just remember. I'll answer the radio. And you tend to the driving."

I tried not to be nervous. His driving was all right but I was aware he was hot to go, just like I was many years back. Our first call came. "Unit Ten, Mercy Hospital. A man cut." I had the mike in my hand ready to acknowledge to the dispatcher we had received the call. I saw Pat's hand go for the toggle switch to turn on the red lights and siren.

I pushed his hand. "No red lights or siren. The guy is already cut and he's in the hospital. We're in no hurry." I advised the dispatcher we received the call and were on our way.

We parked next to the emergency room. Pat jumped from the car and was running for the entrance. I shouted, "Slow down. I told you, there's no hurry." He stopped and waited for me. I picked up the report board and we walked in.

The nurse at the desk waved us through. A doctor and two nurses were working on a man lying on the operating table. Pat nudged me. "Are we allowed in here while they're treating him?"

"Yes, we have to. There's a chance he might die. We have to find out what happened. Did you ever hear of a dying declaration?"

"Yeah, that's strong evidence when you go to court. The jury believes a man won't lie if he knows he's dying."

I walked to the other side of the table so I wouldn't be in the way. The doctor looked up and nodded his head.

I smiled at him and asked if it was all right to talk to the victim. He nodded his head yes. I looked and saw the man's throat had been cut from ear to ear. Pat leaned over my shoulder to get a look. He made a gagging sound and shouted, "Holy shit." He picked up a waste basket and stuck his head into it. The doctor and two nurses smiled.

The doctor muttered through his mask, "New man?"

"Yeah. We all go through it." I finished my report and went to the car. Pat was sitting in the passenger side staring out the window. I got in and he didn't say anything. I drove a couple blocks and he looked at me. "I'm sorry, Bob. I really messed up in there. I made a real ass out of myself. I think I'm going to quit. I can't hack that gory crap."

"It will be all right. Don't worry about it. A few more calls and it won't bother you. A little blood won't hurt you. The only time you worry about blood is if it's yours. Come on now, forget it. Let's get something to eat. I know a place where they got the best chili."

His eyes opened wide, and his cheeks ballooned. He flung open the door and his upper body hung out. "You rotten son of ahhhh."

Two months later I was promoted to detective. I was assigned to the Homicide Squad. I didn't hear from Pat Mc Carthy for about a year. The dispatcher gave me an assignment to go to the High Level Bridge where a man had jumped, missed the water and landed on the railroad tracks.

I no sooner acknowledged receiving the assignment and was on the way when a familiar voice came over the radio. It was Pat Mc Carthy. He shouted, "Hurry, Bob!"

I grabbed the mike and shouted. "If that man is still alive, get an ambulance and transport him to the hospital."

"He's not alive. I'll show you when you get here." I thought to myself what now?

I parked on a hill overlooking the tracks. I could see Mc Carthy and his partner standing over a blanket. Pat spotted me and motioned for me to hurry. I ran down to them.

"What the hell is going on? Why are you so excited?"

Pat pointed to the highest part of the bridge, "He jumped from up there, and landed here on the tracks."

I stared at him with a puzzled look, "So what are you trying to tell me?"

He pulled the blanket off the body. It was twisted and busted up. I just stared at Mc Carthy.

"Don't you see, Bob? His watch. It's a Timex. Remember the commercial with John Cameron Swayze when he use to say, "A Timex takes a lickin and keeps on tickin."

I shook my head. "Would you like to get that chili now?"

A Rude Awakening

When a veteran officer gets close to retirement he wants to make sure nothing jeopardizes it. The one person who could ruin it and possibly get him killed is a rookie. In their eagerness they run into dangerous situations without thinking. When they turn on the red lights and siren they take too many chances. In order to protect himself the older officer will make the decisions and drive the car. The story I am going to tell is a little different. Harry Werful had a couple of weeks before retirement and all he wanted to do was nothing. Let the rookie do it all.

Jim looked at his partner at roll call for the midnight shift. Old Harry had the same tired look on his face that he had seen many times before. He was getting ready for retirement and just wanted to coast through his last days. Jim was an eager young officer who wanted action. He knew the first thing after roll call Harry would get in the passenger side of the scout car. He would have no choice but to drive the whole shift.

He got in the driver side and started up the car. He looked over at his partner with a disgusted look. Old Harry was turning down his hearing aid so the radio wouldn't wake him up when he fell asleep. He looked at the rookie.

185

"I'm so lucky Jim to have a partner with your young eyes, and good reflexes. A driver that I can put my life in his hands every night. I really trust you, son."

"Knock off the bullshit Harry. I heard it before. You're a short timer. When I get your age I can get a young chauffeur. You told me that crap before. Don't tell me again."

He drove to their district. Harry looked over at him. "You're the best partner on the department Jim. I'm really fortunate to have you." Jim just rolled his eyes. "Now I'm just going to put my head back for a short time. If anything comes up be sure to call me."

"How the hell are you going to hear me? You turned down your hearing aid." Jim felt the hair rise on the back of his neck. He thought, it will be a relief when he does retire.

Three in the morning and they answered five calls. It was amazing how fast Harry could get back to sleep when they returned to the car. Jim drove through the dark alleys looking for break-ins to the buildings between calls. He looked over at Harry. His head was leaning so far back it looked like it was going to crack off and drop into the back seat. Jim thought if there were any burglars working these alleys they'd be scared off by Harry's loud snoring. The more he looked at him sleeping the more disgusted he got. He shook his head, then he got an idea.

He drove out of the alley onto Front Street. There were divider bumps in the middle of it. Jim sped up the car and drove two miles over the bumps. Harry's head jerked up and down but he didn't wake up. Jim couldn't believe anyone could sleep through that jarring.

He drove to the end of Front Street where the railroad trains do their switching. It was a dark area that smelled strongly of diesel exhaust. The only lights were on the front of the huge engines. Jim saw one of them idling about twenty feet off the road. He parked the scout car, got out and slammed the door as hard as he could. It didn't faze Harry. He slept on.

The engineer leaned out the window and watched the policeman walk up to him. "Can I help you officer?"

"You sure can." He then explained what he wanted. The engineer smiled and nodded.

Jim got back into the car. Again he slammed the door. Harry kept right on sleeping and snoring. Jim drove the scout car up onto the tracks. The large diesel engine slowly crept closer to the car. When it got about five feet away it stopped. The powerful light on it illuminated the whole inside of the car. It was brighter then daylight. Harry's head was still leaning over the seat silhouetted in front of the huge light.

Jim put his arm out the window and pumped it up and down. The engineer saw the signal. He revved up the engine and blew the horn. The vibrations from the blast shook the car.

Even in his deep sleep Harry recognized that sound. His head leaped forward, then turned to the right and looked directly into the powerful bright light. The engineer sounded the horn again.

Harry jumped to the left and screamed. "Hit the gas! Get me the hell out of here!" He was crawling over Jim but he got stuck on the steering wheel.

Jim laughed. "Harry if you want to drive just tell me. I'll get on the passenger side."

Never Should Of Took That Stuff

Ben Donaher was a detective who loved his job.
Working the homicide squad made him one of the elite. He
was all business. The suits he wore were the best, and
always pressed, with starched white shirts, conservative
neck ties, and shoes highly polished. The man looked like
the movie star William Holden but taller, and I'm sure a lot
tougher. I was a new detective and glad to be his partner.
Ben had been a detective for twenty years. Through his
knowledge and experience he was an expert in homicide
cases. He taught me a lot.

Ben was always cool and nothing ever seemed to upset
him. I only saw him get mad on one occasion. We were
working on a case where a store clerk had been murdered in
a robbery. We got the name of the suspect from a snitch and
were on our way to find him. I was driving the car and Ben
was reading reports, and looking at pictures of the man we
were looking for. The dispatcher interrupted the silence.
"Unit 712 go to Riverside Hospital, they got two men who
overdosed."

Ben had a questioned look on his face and quickly
grabbed the mike. "Dispatcher this is Unit 712 we're a
homicide unit."

The dispatcher shouted back. "Unit 712 1 know
you are. All the vice and drug units are out-of-service. The
hospital says these guys are in bad shape. We need detectives so you take the call. Go to Riverside Hospital."

Ben didn't answer right away. He shook his head.
"Damn dope heads. Who cares what kind of shape they're
in. The fools did it to themselves. We want to get the
bastard who shot that woman. Just a waste of time fooling
with them jerks."

The dispatcher shouted over the radio. "Unit 712 did
you receive my last transmission?"

Ben cussed a little more then pressed the button on the
mike. "Yea, we received your transmission."

I made a quick U turn and headed for the hospital. Ben
reached over and tapped me on the shoulder. "We're in no
hurry Bob, slow it down. They took the shit let them suffer
the consequences. I have no mercy for them junkies. No
matter what we do for them, they'll just go back taking that
stuff. The poor girl who got killed in that robbery was
trying to make a living. The punk who did it is the one we
want. I just wish I could find a large stash of drugs belong-
ing to some pusher. I would taint it with the most powerful
laxatives. When he sold it to the hop heads they would get
the shits for a month. I'm sure there would be one less
pusher on the streets."

We walked into the emergency room and were met by
the strong smell of disinfectants. Two young men with all
the appearances of hippies were lying unconscious on

guerneys. Ben stared at them and said. "Now there's two fine specimens. I wonder what they owe their success to."

A doctor walked up to us. In his palm were three large white pills. "Here is what we think they took."

I asked. "What are they?"

"Horse tranquilizers, a very strong drug, it can kill a person very easily"

Ben just shook his head and mumbled. "That's what they got dumpsters for."

The doctor gave him a funny look then reached down to adjust the tubes going into the nose of one of the men. The man started to talk. I thought to myself, I bet there was a party and there are more people in bad shape. I bent over close to his ear and asked. "Where was the party? How many people were at the party?" I kept repeating the questions. Finally, he asked.

"You a cop?"

"Yes I'm a cop. Right now I'm not interested in arresting any one. We're concerned that some one might die from those pills you guys were taking. We want to get to the rest of the people."

"Across the street from the shelter house at Wilson Park. The bottom apartment to the duplex. My brother's there."

We quickly ran to our car and drove to Wilson Park. Ben pointed to the only duplex across from the shelter house. "That's the rat's nest." We cupped our hands to the windows and looked inside. There were five unconscious people lying on the floor. Ben contacted the dispatcher and requested back up, and a rescue squad. We kicked in the front door and immediately ran to the bodies and checked for pulses. They were all breathing, but were in a deep sleep.

A skinny guy with long dirty blond hair started to mumble. Ben leaned over him to hear what he was saying. The guy's blood-shot eyes slowly opened. He stared at Ben for a long time then said in a slurred voice. "Who the hell are you looking at?"

Ben replied, "I'm Mr. James Neve from Neve's Funeral Home. You passed away and we're preparing you. Your mother bought you a nice blue serge suit and a bright red necktie. She got the best coffin we have. We're going to give you a bath, and a butch hair cut. You're going to look and smell like a real man when we're done with you."

The guy's eyes came wide open and he screamed. "I knew that shit was no good. Why did I take it. Man I'm dead. I kept telling those guys that shit was no good. Now I'm dead. Man, I'm dead." He kept shaking his head.

Ben put his hands on the guy's head. "Now you can't keep moving like that. We're going to give you a nice hair cut and if you move it won't look good."

"Don't cut my damn hair. I don't want a hair cut."

"Now listen, son, we have to cut your hair. Every coffin we sell we give a free hair cut. So just lay back."

The rescue squad loaded him on a stretcher. He was

still shouting he was dead when they put him in the ambulance. Ben looked at me. "Is there anyone else I should talk with?"

We returned to the hospital for our follow - up report. The doctor who showed us the pills came up to Ben and me. "They look like they'll all make it. Were having trouble with one, though. We can't convince him he's not dead."

BOB MORRISSEY

I Thought I Had Seen It All

The nurses and doctors from Mercy Hospital emergency room were all gathered by the door. I shook their hands and bid them farewell. They knew this was my last night as a police officer. When I hit off in the morning I would start my retirement.

I stood in the dimly lighted driveway of the hospital and took a deep breath. I thought as I looked at the entrance to the emergency room --- I wonder how many times over the years I went through that door. It seems just like yesterday I went on my first investigation here at Mercy Hospital. I can still remember the details. I was a new detective and a hoodlum had been shot in the chest. He didn't want to give me any information concerning the shooting. I knew he saw who shot him because there were powder burns around the wound. This indicated he was shot at close range.

I was determined to clear this case. I was not going to have my first investigation go unsolved. I looked him straight in the eyes and said. "The surgeon who is going to operate on you has very bad eye sight. He loses about ninety five percent of the people he operates on. You better be prepared to meet your maker. The lord is going to ask why you lied to that detective back on earth, when you only had a few hours to live."

He stuttered, and mumbled a little then told me who had shot him. I was unaware that the surgeon who was going to operate was standing near and heard the whole conversation. Needless to say I had to give him and the Chief an explanation.

It was now 2:30 in the morning. Driving back to the station I was laughing to myself thinking of all the crazy things that had happened over thirty three years. At Monroe and 17th street my mind flashed back to reality. My head did a double take as a station wagon drove past me from the opposite direction. On the roof tied to the luggage rack was a body spread-eagled. I made a quick U-turn and grabbed the mike. "Dispatcher this is Unit 812. I'm following a station wagon with Ohio plates 2311 BL, north on Monroe St. It has a human body on the roof. Send me a marked unit to pull it over."

I kept following the car and in the matter of a couple of minutes I saw red lights flashing in my rear view mirror. A few blocks ahead other police cruisers with red lights flashing were coming to my assistance.

The scout car that was behind me passed at a high rate of speed. When it got next to the station wagon an officer motioned with a bright spot light to pull over. The other cruisers boxed it in. The brake lights of the station went on and it stopped.

I jumped from the car, with my gun in hand, and ran to the station wagon. The driver pushed both his hands out the window so I could see them. He shouted. "Officers, wait this is not what it looks like. I can explain."

I shouted, "Go ahead."

"You see officers this is my best friend up on the roof. We were at a party and the damn fool got drunk, and sick. I just bought this car and I didn't want him to throw up on my new upholstery. I tied him up there, and if he pukes I won't have a problem. I'll drive to a U-Do-It car wash and I'll spray him, and my car off."

I looked at the uniformed officers. "This one's yours boys. This old man is retiring."

BOB MORRISSEY

Still A Peace Officer

What a beautiful day. The waves were rolling in and the breeze was refreshing. I thought what a wonderful feeling, retired and walking this peaceful beach in Florida. What a contrast from past years where people were in constant conflict trying to hurt one another. As a police officer I was paid to put a stop to fighting and try to make people live in harmony. I was glad those days were over. I hoped to live the remainder of my life in this paradise just being quiet and tranquil. No more watching people in pain from being shot, stabbed, or from automobile accidents. That mess was behind me.

I continued my quiet walk with a large contented smile. It was good to be alive. I felt so relaxed. This is the way life was meant to be.

As luck would have it, sounds of the past pierced my ears. "You rotten old bastard you can't fish here. This area of the beach is for swimmers and surfers. Get your pole and get the hell out of here." I looked up and saw five teen-age boys surrounding an elderly man. The man brandished a long plastic pipe in his hand. He was shouting.

"I was down here at six o'clock this morning. This is where I fish. I'm not moving and any of you punks try to make me move I'll break this over your damn head."

I tried to walk by without saying anything. Then I thought someone is going to get hurt here. Maybe I should walk up the beach, call the police and let them handle it. But, by the time the police get here this will turn physical. I had mixed feelings about intervening. I felt I had to do something to put a stop to this. I stood and stared at what was going on. One of the teen-aged boys turned around, looked at me and in a sharp voice shouted, "What's your problem?"

"I got a big problem and I thought you guys might help."

"What the hell is your problem? Do you know this crazy old coot?"

"No I don't know the man. My problem is about two miles up the beach. I came across a large yellow water proof plastic bag that washed up on the shore. It has tape wrapped around it with foreign writing on it. I believe there is marijuana inside that bag. I didn't open it because I never saw marijuana. I'm on my way to call the police but I didn't want to bother them if it isn't marijuana. I was going to find someone who knows what it looks like, then call the police.

The argument stopped immediately. All eyes were on me. The boys had serious looks and were now surrounding me. One of them said in a tone dripping with respect. "Sir, you don't have to call the police. We know what weed, I mean marijuana looks like. Just tell us where you saw it and

200

we'll go check it out. If it's marijuana we'll call the police."

"I sure hate to bother you boys. And I appreciate this. I didn't want to call the police if it turned out not to be marijuana."

"Oh sir, you're not bothering us. Just tell us where it is and we'll take care of it. It's no problem, believe me."

"Well it's about two miles up the beach. You see that large palm tree? The bag is about a hundred yards south of it."

No more words were said. The race was on. Five teenage boys running toward the large tree. The old man turned to me. He must not a' heard what I told the boys.

"What did you tell those guys to make them get out of here so fast?"

"I told them if they didn't quit bothering you and get the hell out of here right now, I would kick their asses."

He stared at me with a strange expression. "You don't look that tough. How old are you?"

If you liked this book, why not order one for a friend?

Humorous Beat: Actual Police Stories
Officer Bob Morrissey ISBN:0-9707560-3-8

_____ Copies @ $13.95 each _____

% Sales tax (Florida only) _____

Shipping and Handling $4.00 each _____

Total: _____

Check or money order in the full amount must accompany this order.

For autographed copies mail to:
Bob Morrissey
8286 Spicebush Terrace
Port St. Lucie, FL 34952
Tel: (772) 879-3958

Send To:
Name_____

Address _____

City, State, Zip Code _____

_____

Phone Number (____)____-_____

HUMOROUS BEAT

If you liked this book, why not order one for a friend?

Humorous Beat: Actual Police Stories
Officer Bob Morrissey ISBN:0-9707560-3-8

_____ Copies @ $13.95 each _____
6% Sales tax (Florida only) _____
Shipping and Handling $4.00 _____
Total: _____

Check or money order in the full amount must accompany this order.

For autographed copies mail to:
Bob Morrissey
8286 Spicebush Terrace
Port St. Lucie, FL 34952
Tel: (772) 879-3958

Send To:
Name_____
Address _____
City, State, Zip Code _____

_____
Phone Number (_____)_____-_____

CPSIA information can be obtained
at www.ICGtesting.com
Printed in the USA
FFOW03n0432080117
31054FF